UNVEILED SECRETS

UNVEILED SECRETS

A WEDDING PLANNER MYSTERY

MARY KARNES

This book is dedicated to my children, Tyler, Kathleen, Maggie, Rob, Tom, Tess, and Julia; half by birth, half by marriage. How lucky am I?

Chapter One

Will you want to preserve your bridal bouquet? There are many ways to do so. You can dry the whole thing, dry just a few petals, or send in a photo of the fresh bouquet and commission a mini painting of it. Etsy has many such affordable options.

To say that I was surprised would be an understatement. My old, well, my long-time friend, Charlie Wentworth, was getting married. We lived in a small town, and I didn't even know he was dating anyone…no one did.

He had asked me to plan it, and I had mixed emotions. Of course, I would. He had done a lot to help me legally in the past (yes, I had had a few run-ins with the law in the past couple of years) and I would return the favor with my own set of skills, ha ha. I wouldn't even charge him. I pushed down the questions in the back of my brain as to why I felt discombobulated at the thought of Charlie getting married. I acknowledged that he had always had a soft spot for me, and although my feelings weren't the same, maybe, just maybe, I had always thought of him as a back-up.

My current love life? I was back together with my old boyfriend, Brian McAllister, high school heartthrob and love of my life. I was a recent divorcée from Southern California, being forced from my marriage and my home, when my cheating ex took up with my next-door neighbor. I ran home to my roots here in New England with my sixteen-year-old daughter in tow. Everything was going well, my business as a wedding planner was blooming, and then, last year, I was accused of killing my favorite florist. Let me clarify, my favorite florist, but not my favorite person. Even *I* had to agree that I looked like a great suspect. Charlie was there for me, represented me as my attorney. I slightly took advantage of his lingering adolescent feelings for me, refusing to consider that I had similar ones. Did I? Or was I just out of sorts because someone I had always thought I could count on day or night would be unavailable after he got married and had a family of his own to answer to. Charlie had made it very clear that he and Remley would be trying for a family asap. Uuuuuggg…TMI!!

We were meeting today in my Main Street office to talk about the wedding, and I would have the pleasure of meeting "Rem," as Charlie referred to her, with oh so much affection.

My office was on the second floor of a historic house renovated for commercial use. On the first floor was "The Perk," everyone's favorite coffee hangout, and owned by my best friend since forever, Jen Cooper. I'm proud to say I was now able to pay her full retail rate rent for my upstairs office space. Jen had generously rented me my office for less than nothing when I first came back home. And sadly, I had to accept her help.

Oh, she said the space was empty anyway, but both she and I knew that she could rent it in a heartbeat after her most recent tenant had moved out. Lucky me that the vacancy opened when it did. I moved into my historic home, purchased from my half of the sale of my outrageously expensive tiny California marital home, on a Tuesday and into my new office space the next day. I jumped into the wedding planning business with both feet; it was my way to support myself and my daughter, Ellis. Grant, my ex, did help some. Wedding planning had been a part-time gig in California, but was my life's blood here.

"Knock, knock," Charlie tapped on my half-open door, as he entered my space with a pretty, young woman following closely on his heels. Okay, now to stare and get a full description so I could share with Jen and Sarah when we met for coffee later. Jen, the aforementioned best friend, and Sarah…well, she is a bit more complicated. Sometimes I just love her, more often I hate her. Can you say, 'there's history there.'

Remley was a tall brunette with a pixie cut and big blue eyes. She had the look of a young Audrey Hepburn, and…looked more than a little like me. I think the Audrey Hepburn vibe was intentional; she was dressed in a sleeveless classic black shift dress. We made eye contact, and she gave me a shy smile.

I rose from the guest chair I had been waiting for them in the reception area. Reception area…sounds fancy, it was not. I had two rooms in my rented 'suite'—and a powder room. The room where I now greeted Charlie and Remley was the room that opened from the upstairs hallway. It was pleasantly furnished with two small powder blue guest chairs, a small round table, which typically held wedding-themed coffee table books and fresh flowers. There were two windows, which looked out over the Connecticut River, and they had dusky-blue valences to add a little style. The fabric matched that of my guest chairs. Yes, I did fork over the money to decorate my two-room suite. One had to look prosperous to appeal to potential clients, or so I told myself as I approved the purchase of my décor items.

I gave Charlie an affectionate loose hug and extended my hand to Remley. I smiled broadly as I shook her hand. "So lovely to meet you, Remley. Charlie can't stop raving about you," I said. Remley looked to Charlie and smiled.

"Come in, come in," I ushered them into my inner office and into the guest chairs, which matched the ones in the outer room. I offered them coffee from my little coffee bar and prized espresso machine (please don't tell Jen) they declined. I sat down in my office chair behind my desk and smiled at them. They both seemed nervous. "First of all, congratulations! Have you thought of a date yet?"

They looked at each other and smiled. "We are hoping for Valentine's Day," Remley shared. I could see her squeeze Charlie's hand.

"That's lovely, and here in New England, it's not a popular day because it's in the heart of winter."

"The wedding will be small. I was thinking of something at the club." Charlie was referring to the Eastbury Country Club. A beautiful, rather rustic course, right here in town.

"That shouldn't be too hard to book. If you want, I can reach out to the head of banquet services and see if they have an opening that day."

"Sounds good, Kate, but now Rem and I need to get to our engagement photo shoot."

I stood as well. What? We had so much to discuss! "Jeeze, Charlie, there's still a lot to go over."

"Well, I just thought once we had the club booked, we were all set."

Oh, my stars! "No, that's just scratching the surface. We have to book entertainment, a florist, videographer, schedule appointments for Remley's dress, hair, and makeup…this is just the beginning."

"That's why we have you, right, Kate!" Charlie all of a sudden seemed rushed and stressed. He couldn't get out of my office fast enough. He didn't wait for a reply from me, but marched Remley to the reception room and went for the exterior door.

"Wait," I squeaked out. "I shoved one of my business cards with all my contact info into Remley's hand. "Call me and we will have lunch without party pooper Charlie," I said with a smile to soften my words.

Remley smiled, but she too felt the shift in Charlie's demeanor and just gave me a quick nod.

Weird. I shrugged it off and decided to go grab a cup of coffee downstairs at The Perk. I texted Sarah on the way. I know, not the wisest to text and walk downstairs.

Me—*Meet at Jen's for coffee in 5?*

Sarah—*You bet*

I entered The Perk through the interior entrance (down the staircase outside my office door and into the main room of the coffee shop) and grabbed a table right away. It was mid-morning, but The Perk was still very busy. Tally, Jen's number one barista and assistant store manager, smiled a 'hello,' gave me a wink, and started in on my beverage. I have never paid for a cup of coffee in my life at Jen's, but I hope I more than made up for that in tips to the staff. Jen came into the main room from the back, carrying a tray of baked goods to be stocked under glass domes by the register, and saw me. She too smiled and mouthed, "Two minutes." I smiled back.

"Kate," Tally sang out, indicating my drink was ready at the bar. I took it from her outstretched hand.

"Thanks, Tally, I slipped a five in the tip jar. "Sarah's on her way; I pulled another ten out of my cross-body bag and handed it to her. Would you please make her favorite, my treat."

Tally justifiably raised her eyebrows at me as she nodded and went about making the beverage. Yes, it was safe to say that Sarah and I had not even been civil to each other in the past. But in the last year, she had won my respect, if not my total faith in her. We had a lot of bad history, mainly centered around Brian, my old and new love. Brian had been Sarah's first in high school, and he was still a sore point. Did I steal him from her? Kinda, but not completely. Confusing, I know.

Speak of the devil, in walked Sarah Deloro. She was tall, blond, thin, and beautiful. Today she wore tan worsted slacks, a cream blouse, and a Hermes scarf tied around her neck. No matter what, I doubt I could ever duplicate the knot on that scarf. That knowledge helped me not covet it.

When I wasn't impressed with her business acumen (she was Connecticut's top realtor), and intelligence, I kinda hated her. The feeling was mutual. I had finally forgiven her for her betrayal of a mutual client last spring. The encounter had taught me a couple of things: 1) I could *never* completely trust Sarah Deloro, and somehow, we would always seem to come back together. I'm really not sure why.

"What's up, Manet?" No smile, Sarah slid into one of the two open chairs at my table. She still sometimes called me by my maiden name.

"Sarah!" Tally chose that moment to call her name and announce her beverage was ready.

"Ah, you bought me a coffee, you're getting soft, Manet." Sarah rose gracefully and retrieved her coffee. She took a hesitant sip. "Just the way I like it, thanks, Katie." And this time she did smile.

Jen joined us, bringing her own coffee and a plate of brownies, my kryptonite.

"Hey, ladies." Jen looked tired. I knew she had the early shift today, arriving at 4:30 AM, yikes! "What's up, Katie? Why the pow wow?"

"Yeah, Manet, what's up?" Oh, Sarah, we were so complicated in our friendship. But she had a good pulse on the community, and she and Jen were very good friends. That relationship had blossomed when I was out west before I moved back home. Hey, if you can't beat 'em, join 'em.

"Guess who's wedding I'm doing in the spring?"

"Charlie Wentworth's," Sarah said without batting an eye.

"No way," Jen responded, looking from Sarah to me.

See what I mean about Sarah and her pulse on the community? She knew all, I kid you not.

"Okay, I'll bite," I said. "How did you know about Charlie and Remley?"

"Remley!" Jen said around her bite of brownie. "What kind of name is 'Remley' and who is she anyway?

We both ignored poor Jen. "Charlie approached me about a listing by the country club, the old Weatherford place. He said he was interested in buying it for his 'bride.'"

"Wow," I said, taking my own bite of brownie, quickly breaking my self-imposed pledge to eat better, "Charlie must be doing better than I thought. I heard about all the renovations the previous owner did before he was transferred to Boston and had to put the house on the market. "It's huge!" I enthused.

"You're right there, Katie. There's the main house, a guest house, and the property also has some acreage, horse property. Asking price is five point two million." Nice payday for Sarah! She had sold the property to the previous owners, too. "Apparently, the new bride is from Kentucky and is horse mad."

"Funny, I didn't get any type of accent there."

"Probably wouldn't. According to Charlie, she was shipped off to boarding school at the age of eight, first to England, then to Switzerland. Back here to the states for college."

"How did they meet?" I was so curious.

"I hinted around to find out," Sarah said around another bite of brownie, but neither shared. If I had to guess, I'd say undergrad. I do know they both went to Georgetown, but didn't discuss any 'good old times' when I was around. They were pretty quiet, actually, although they are very excited about the property. Have lots of ideas for it."

"Do you…" Well, this was awkward. I started again. "Do you think she was contributing to the property purchase, or was Charlie footing the whole bill?"

Neither Sarah nor Jen batted an eye at my rather indelicate question. "Charlie was the only one on the pre-authorization letter provided by his lender. And he *was* putting down about 50%." I have to say I was surprised at Sarah sharing this financial information. She rarely did. I guess she thought I was privy to Charlie's financials, as I was his planner.

Sarah, who knew most people's net worth in town as she handled their home purchases, shared her surprise. "My guess is that the purchase is a little rich for Charlie's blood. But I've never sold him a home before, so what do I know? Maybe he has made some good investments?" Her sentence ended in a question. She wasn't convinced.

Chapter Two

If you're using escort cards as seating assignments, try to set them up inside, as one little gust of wind will send them all askew. Better yet, think about an alternative style of sharing guest table assignments—think writing table numbers on a mirror or a professionally created chart.

I took the last slug of coffee in one gulp. "Well, ladies, I have to go. If you think of anything fun to share, let me know." I picked up my pocketbook and stood.

Why the rush, Katie, hot date?" Sarah asked with a snark. And…we're back. Even if we are friends, and it's only been in the recent year that we have become kind of….friends. That doesn't mean we don't pick at each other.

"Actually, yes," and I smiled a little smugly.

"Yeah?" She stood too. Jen was watching the back and forth between us like a pickleball match. "Me too." Whaaaaat?? My little brain screamed.

"What the heck, Sarah?" Both Jen and I said at the same time. We looked at each other and smiled. I sat back down. "Spill!" I ordered. Sarah sat down as well.

Was Sarah Deloro blushing? Yes, I think she was. Her unlined face, she didn't have children, was getting the shade of a pink carnation.

Both Jen and I *did* have kids, so we just sat there, knowing that our silence would break her and get her to tell all. Well, at least a little bit. We leaned into her.

Sarah leaned back, "Okay, okay!" And she giggled. She *giggled.* Will wonders never cease?

"His name is Leland Rosetti. He was a cardiologist in Boston, but he was looking for a quieter life and wanted to move here, work in Hartford. I helped him find a house." Sarah was quiet then and looked down at her coffee." We all were quiet for a moment, then Jen whooped. Yep, she did. I couldn't be left out, so I whooped too. A few customers looked over at our table, but when they realized there really wasn't much to see, they went back to their own conversations.

"Maybe Brian and I can have a little peace now," I teased. Too far? But Sarah just grinned. Okay, she had it bad. "Free wedding planning, Deloro."

"Whoo, hoo!" Sarah burst out. "You're my witness, Jen. I am going to be the biggest bridezilla, Kate!" I didn't doubt it. She was a friendzilla already. But Sarah and I have had our good times, as well as our bad. She was a badass, and I'd trust her with my life, I already had.

"What's up tonight?" Jen asked, looking at me. Ah Jen. She was the best friend a girl could have. She had been my number one since we were in elementary school. I didn't hold it against Jen that she and Sarah had gotten close when I was living in California. I was close to Sarah myself, in our own way.

"Brian is taking me to dinner at Jax Downtown, and he said to 'dress up.' I'm looking forward to a big old steak," I laughed. But I hoped my two friends didn't hear the hollow ring in my laugh. I was nervous. Brian had been dropping hints lately. He had mentioned us making things official and maybe starting a family. I loved Brian, I did. I *really* did. And while I was ready to commit, was he, really? He was too jealous, maybe too emotionally immature. He was a hot head, acted first, said sorry later. Not a good mode of operation. I had been with a cheater, my ex. While I didn't think Brian would cheat, I wasn't convinced he was ready to commit. And by 'commit' I meant growing up. He had to learn to put someone else's feelings before his. Just because he was angry and wanted to throw things, he had to think how that may affect someone else, mainly me. But I wasn't ready to end it. So, where did that put me? I wanted to put on the brakes, but if I did, would it have to be over? I didn't know how he would react to that.

"Oh, Katie, tell me you have something new to wear. You can't go out dressed…" Sarah waved her hand around to encompass all of me, especially my regular wedding planner uniform of khaki pants, leather flats, a twin sweater set…and pearls, both at my throat and in my ears. What was wrong with my outfit? But of course, I was going to change into a little black dress. I'm proud to say I've lost the weight I'd gained after a nasty bike accident back in California. I still sported the angry red scar where I broke my leg, but it was fading over time. I had just started wearing dresses and skirts again.

I decided to give Sarah the business. "I really don't have time to change today." I chanced a glance at Jen. She knew what I was up to. She hid a smile.

"Katie Manet! You absolutely have to change. If you don't have anything, come to my house and we'll go through my closet!" I would have laughed, but I didn't want to hurt Sarah's feelings. She was actually being…nice. But the chance of me fitting into size 0 Sarah Deloro's clothes was exactly that…zero.

I gave her a big smile. She got it.

"I hate you, Katie, I really do!" I think she was truly miffed.

"Don't be mad, Sarah. I appreciate the offer, but we both know nothing in your closet would fit me."

If I anticipated a polite protest, I'd be disappointed. "Yeah," she agreed. "What are you, a four or…six?" She asked with a little bit of…disgust.

I wouldn't bite. "About," I agreed. And with that, I took my leave. Sarah was Sarah.

* * *

Brian picked me up right on time at our agreed-upon 6:00 pm. He was looking incredibly handsome in khakis (why could *he* wear them, and I couldn't?), a white button-down shirt, and a navy blazer. He smelled of just the right hint of soap, shaving cream…and Brian.

He held me at arm's length after he kissed me hello. "Wow! You look beautiful, Katie!" His appreciation was real. And I'd never get tired of it. And if truth be told, I felt good too. My dress was indeed a size four, but I was darn proud of that. I'd never be a zero like Sarah, but what mattered was that I was happy.

We arrived at Jax Downtown in eight minutes, found parking, and had fifteen minutes to spare. Hartford was a small city, the capital of Connecticut. But it wasn't a thriving city. Once upon a time, way back when I was a girl, it had been. In those days, it was the insurance capital of the world. Now, not so much. There was a large homeless population, as there was in any city, and the murder rate was one of the highest per capita in the country. But I loved it.

Brian opened the door to the restaurant, and a blast of warm air hit us. We entered with anticipation. My mouth watered just entering the door.

Brian walked up to the hostess stand and gave his name. Silence.

Then, "I'm sorry, sir. I don't see a reservation in your name. Could it be under a different name?"

Biran was momentarily nonplussed. "No," he answered with an edge to his voice. It wouldn't be under another name." Uh oh. This wasn't good. I could feel the heat coming off him.

"Well, do you have an open table?

"I'm so sorry sir, but we have a big group tonight, so we don't have a spare table. You're welcome to have a seat at the bar. You can even have dinner service there," She finished hopefully. Her face betrayed her young age with a couple of breakouts on her chin. She looked so uncomfortable, so nervous. I hoped Brian wouldn't be a jerk. Too late.

"No, we don't want to have dinner at the bar." He didn't raise his voice, but his tone was nasty. He turned his back on her and stomped out of the restaurant. I followed, mouthing, "I'm sorry," to the flustered hostess.

"Brian, hey," I quickly walked to catch up with him and grabbed his arm. "What's wrong?"

"What do you mean? What's wrong? I had a reservation, plans." Now he appeared to be angry at me. I walked past him and headed toward our parking. This behavior was wearing thin. I'd had it with his temper. He finally tried to apologize when we were almost home, but the mood was spoiled.

Brian tried to make amends with a quick drive-through at McDonald's. It wasn't Jax Downtown, but it was almost as good. I am a simple woman. He got a Big Mac Meal, large, and I got an order of fries, large, and a coffee *with* cream. There are few things I liked better than French fires, and Brian, tonight, was not one of them. But he did come a long way in the make-up department with this little stop. We even had a good laugh and a sentimental moment when we reminisced about our high school days in this every parking lot. Well, the parking lot had been repaved and expanded over the years, but still.

He dropped me off at my house. I didn't ask him in. More time to work on Charlie and Remley's wedding, I told myself.

* * *

I went into the house and headed straight to my home office. My historic home had twin parlors. When one entered the house, one stood in a roomy foyer with one parlor to the right, which Ellis, my sixteen-year-old daughter, and I used as a family room. The parlor to the left served as my home office. Ellis had a late volleyball practice, so I had the house to myself. I switched on the light in my office and sat down at my desk. I loved my home office. It was painted blue, like my space downtown. I had a sturdy desk that fit with the historic architecture of the house. My desk chair was purchased from Costco, and I had all manner of wedding items on shelves on the walls: idea books, fabric samples, vision boards, dried flowers. But my favorite thing, (and I had a matching one in my downtown office), was my chaise lounge. And yes, of course, I've been known to take a nap or two on it. I had a lovely blue cashmere throw to wrap up with. But I didn't feel like a nap now, I was too keyed up. Brian was going through something. And he was pulling me down with him. I was ready and able to support him, but he had to share with me first. And any time I asked him how he was doing, he became defensive.

I had sunk into my Costco chair and put my head down on my desk, but sat up just as quickly. I wasn't going to feel sorry for myself. I was going to be productive. And I was just that. I picked out my favorite vendors for Charlie and Remley's wedding. The vendor I was most excited about was the photographer. While not new to the photography world, he was new to me. We had worked together at a wedding last month, and I was very impressed, although if I was honest, he was a bit moody. I fired off an email with the date, venue, and Charlie and Remley's names. Hopefully, he'd get back to me soon. I wanted to get all the vendors booked asap. I paused a moment. Would they have preferred to have our good mutual friend, Addalee, be the photographer? No, I assured myself, she would want to attend as a guest.

Chapter Three

If you're having a plated meal, write the guests' protein choice on the back of their place card for ease of serving. No place card? Give the same information to the caterer with a table map.

I had a call with Clyde this morning, the 'new to me' photographer, who I was hoping to book for Charlie and Remley's wedding. I needed to get out of the house, so after I got Ellis off to school, I headed downtown to my Main Street office.

I unlocked my outer office door, shrugged out of my trench coat, hung it on the coat tree, and went into my inner space. I threw my bag on the chaise lounge, then settled into the office chair behind my desk before I picked up my iPhone to call Clyde.

I scrolled to his contact info and hit 'call.' He picked up on the second ring.

"Hey, Clyde, it's Kate Ludlow from Mother of the Bride." I always tried to sound positive and upbeat.

"Hey Kate! I was just going to call you, one of your couples booked me a couple days ago. We actually did the engagement shoot yesterday. I had a cancellation, and they jumped on it."

Wow! Could it be Charlie and Remley? That Remley would have to be watched. She was more of a type A person than I had figured. Sometimes those brides proved to be problematic. I wasn't holding the keys to planning or vendors, but I liked to be kept in the loop.

I smiled before I answered, hoping my irritation wouldn't appear in my voice. "Let me guess, Charlie and Remley?"

"Bingo," Clyde answered. "A nice couple, although I thought I'd hear from you first."

"No worries, but I sure would appreciate it if you'd keep me in the loop going forward."

"Understood, Kate. That makes it easier for me, too." We signed off, promising to chat soon about 'First Look' possibilities, 'Golden Hour' sites, and so forth. The 'First Look' is when the Groom sees his Bride before the wedding ceremony. This is not always done. Some couples wish to wait for the 'wow' moment when the bride makes her entrance, and she walks down the aisle during the wedding ceremony. Other couples want to be efficient and get as many photos as possible out of the way before the ceremony. The 'Golden Hour' is that magical time, approximately thirty minutes before the official setting of the sun. The light is well…golden. And some of my favorite photos were captured at this photo shoot. But one has to have a plan when (on the wedding timeline) and where these photo opportunities will take place. Thus, extensive discussion with the photographer is needed.

* * *

Ellis had been a particularly surly teen the next morning as she headed to school. She was picked up this morning, just like every morning, by her boyfriend, Kevin. Kevin was a great kid, the son of my old high school chum Rainey. She had her hands full with a college freshman, as well as a senior, junior (Kevin) and a sophomore in high school—all boys. I'm not saying Kevin doesn't bear watching. He was a hormonal teen boy, after all. It was up to me to put the fear of God into him. I did and would continue to do so. Hey, I came by it honestly; my mom did the same to Brian when we were in high school, back in the day.

The only downside to the Ellis/Kevin relationship was that I didn't see as much of Ellis' old gang, composed of lacrosse-playing Candy, cheerleading Whitney, and super-smart Peter, as I used to. I missed them and imagined Ellis did too. I would have to put a bug in her ear to not forget her friends.

Let's just say this morning, I need a good, strong cup of the nectar of the gods, coffee, more than usual. I decided to forego my mom's old percolator on my stove top, as well as my new, state-of-the-art espresso machine. I would head to Jen's shop. Hopefully, she would have a spare minute or two to chat. She had two daughters, one a year younger and one a year older than Ellis. She'd get me.

* * *

It was a little blustery this morning, and I was regretting my decision to walk. I had on my LL Bean 'Bean Boots,' well worn-in, of course, jeans, purchased off the TikTok Shop, and a button-down shirt with a down vest over it. Wish I had grabbed a mid-weight jacket. Oh well. I entered Jen's shop to warmth and the heavenly smell of coffee and baked goods.

I scanned the coffee bar for Jen, but didn't see her. Tally, Jen's right-hand, tipped her head to the right. I smiled my thanks and found Jen seated, not the norm, with Sarah. They were in deep conversation. What was up?

I joined them, pulling out the extra chair that was at their table, and took a seat. "Ladies," I greeted them. They looked up at me with sad, distracted eyes

"What's going on?" It was obvious that something was, and not the good kind of something.

Jen put her hand over mine, which I had placed on the tabletop. "You haven't heard, Katie?" There was concern in her voice, and her eyes.

"Oh, God! What's happened?

"Don't panic, Manet." Leave it to Sarah to let me know right off it wasn't something to do with Ellis, or anyone in my tight circle. I always knew she was being snarky when she called me 'Manet, ' my maiden name. But she still left it to Jen to tell me the bad news.

"There's been a murder," Jen said in almost a whisper, but with deep emotion.

What the heck? "A murder?" I repeated.

"I think you know him, or knew him," Jen corrected herself.

My heart sank into the pit of my stomach. Oh my God. "Katie, let me get you some water," Jen said as she jumped up and ran to the coffee bar.

Sarah put her hand on my forearm in an unlikely Sarah gesture. I don't think she has ever touched me in anything but anger before. "Katie, it's okay. No one close. Sorry we gave you a fright."

Jen had returned with a paper cup of water and was moving it toward my mouth as if to feed me like a toddler.

"Jen!" I said more harshly than I intended. She looked crestfallen, but stopped her procession toward me with the water. "Sit." I softly commanded. She complied.

I turned my eyes to Sarah. "Who?" We had had our share of losses in our little town recently.

"Clyde Bunker, the photographer," Sarah said softly.

"Are you kidding me? I just talked to him yesterday. He was going to do Charlie and Remley's wedding for us!" I was horrified. "How?" I asked.

Jen and Sarah looked at each other. "It's pretty gruesome," Jen whispered. Yes, it was true. We were getting some attention from the other patrons. "Are you sure you don't want to have a sip of water first, or drink your coffee?" She indicated the cappuccino Tally had given me.

"No, I don't want a sip of water or coffee, I snapped." And immediately felt awful. "Sorry," I said contritely and looked at both Jen and Sarah. "Just tell me, please."

"He was shot with an arrow!" Jen said almost gleefully. I don't know what it was about Jen. She was the sweetest person in the whole world, but she seemed to get some sort of thrill about the gory details surrounding people's deaths. She was the first to comment about a nasty car accident and fill in all the details. Take the murder of our town's favorite florist last year. She was all over that one like a baby stuck to its mama in a crowded county fair.

But still, she shocked me. "An arrow!" I said much too loudly, and several heads turned again to stare at our little group of three. How in the heck did *that* happen?

"Is it?" I paused. "Is it really *murder?*"

Jen snorted and honked a laugh. Jen! I thought. "I'd imagine so, shot through with an arrow, and left for dead by his car at his condo."

I looked at Sarah, and she was giving Jen the eye roll, too. We would have to calm her down.

"Take a breath, Cooper," Sarah said to Jen in a tone she usually reserved for me. Although she used Jen's married name, not her maiden one.

"Sorry," Jen looked around to see if people were noticing her, they were. "Oops," she said, looking down at her hands on the table. "I don't know why I get so wound up about this stuff. It's not like I like it or anything." Wasn't it, I thought? She loved gory movies and action shoot 'em ups. I guess we all had our things. Jen just didn't want to accept that this was hers.

I turned to Sarah. She would be the more reliable source. "He was seriously shot with an arrow and left for dead at his condo, out by his car?" I was horrified, and I think I sounded like it.

Sarah was going to enjoy her time in the spotlight. She was a glory hound after all. I could tell she couldn't wait to share the details. "Mrs. Richards, from the bookstore, found him about midnight by his car. She had been at her daughter Shelly's. Shelly had just given birth to her second baby, and Mrs. Richards was helping, but last night she really wanted to sleep in her own bed. She said she came home after the baby's eleven o'clock feeding. She said, according to the gossip mill, that Clyde had his car door open, and was half inside and half out, and he had bled out. The arrow was right through his chest. A clean shot if there ever was one."

How awful. "Do they have any suspects?" I asked Sarah. Why would anyone want to kill Clyde? He was fairly new to the area; certainly he hadn't done anything yet to make someone *that* mad. I joked with myself. I was as bad as Jen.

Jen picked up here. "No suspects. They're doing the autopsy today, but it's pretty obvious what the cause of death was, and I'm sure the 'manner' of death will be murder." Someone had been watching her *Law and Order*. Jen had all the lingo down.

It dawned on me then. Charlie and Remley had their engagement shoot yesterday. I wonder if they had any insight into what was going to happen. Probably not, but I was going to poke around.

"Katie, Katie!" Jen said, snapping me out of my thoughts. "I know that look you're thinking, Remley and Charlie might know something, and you're scheming on how to get it out of them without being too obvious, aren't you?" The disapproving look on her face cut into me a bit.

"Of course she is, Jen." I wasn't sure if Sarah was going to smile indulgently or give me a dirty look. That pretty much defined our relationship.

I pushed my chair back as I drained the last of my cappuccino rather indelicately. "Hey, I have no skin in the game. I hope the police solve this, but I'm out." And I meant it, but did I? There was nothing like the thrill of working on a case. But if I wanted my relationship with Brian to survive, I'd better keep my nose out of it.

I kept putting off facing Brian's short fuse. I knew this was a common complaint from those who loved law enforcement personnel. I really needed to give our relationship some time and thought, if I couldn't live with him the way he was, I had to give him the opportunity to make some changes or move on. But I loved him…and therein lay the problem.

Chapter Four

Make sure you have clearly defined roles for your vendors. This should be determined before the big day. Remember, your wedding planner is top dog. He / She calls the shots. Things will go more smoothly if everyone stays in their lane.

Boy, was I dreading the wedding today. I like to think I am a pretty good judge of character. I do not accept everyone who wants to work with me as a client. Just as I am interviewed by a prospective client, I interview the client at the same time. I calculate if we will be a good team, a good fit. That's a must. We are all different, and I am not always everyone's wedding soulmate.

That's why I was, well, to put it bluntly, crushed when a few issues came up with today's bride in our last few planning sessions. I realized with a heavy heart that she was small and mean. But I would get through the day, I had to. I should have had a heads-up when they scheduled their wedding on a Wednesday.

I had done a wedding at this bride, Amber's, venue before. It was a private, park/camp/recreational center on twenty-plus acres in the nearby town of Ranchington. It had a great lake that made a perfect spot for a 'beach' wedding and a pavilion, which was new, and also a nice ceremony spot. For the reception, there was a covered space with stationary tables and benches. The downside? It was all so spread out. The bride was getting ready in the office by the gate, the groom and groomsmen a mile away in some cabins. The ceremony space was a quarter of a mile from the reception space. The only kitchen on site was a quarter mile from the reception tables. And to make it worse, the kitchen was a snack bar, closed for the day, so really, no kitchen. The caterer would cook in a cook-tent closer to the reception space.

The caterer was the most uncommunicative vendor I've ever worked with. And…she didn't want to do her job, but instead wanted me to set the tables for all the guests. Never have I been asked to do that. But to put the cherry on top, she didn't know where the rental company had placed all the China, silverware, glassware, and linens that *she* had ordered and were under her jurisdiction, and had been delivered the evening before.

So…first things first, we had to go find the rentals. Best bet it had been stashed in the snack bar/kitchen. I drove up there, and sure enough, all the rentals were present and accounted for in all their plastic-wrapped glory. Now, how did we get the rentals down to the reception space? I quickly organized a caravan of trucks, good thing the guests who were staying in cabins on site were a truck-driving crowd. They were very good sports and happily chipped in, those who were sober, that is. Many of the guests who were staying on site were already drunk before the ceremony even began. I already had a pit in my stomach. They were ultimately going to be a hard crew to manage; drunken guests always were. I sighed. Next time, I will do a better job of vetting prospective clients. But I shouldn't be so hard on myself. How does one really know? We all wear masks and, at times, hide our true selves, especially if it benefits us.

I was brought out of my melancholy train of thought by the thumping of my watch, indicating an incoming text.

I need a bottle of champagne—From the bride.

Not my job, but happy to help, well, maybe not *happy,* but I'd do it. I had other tasks to attend to.

Where is it located? I queried.

How should I know?—came the rude reply.

It wasn't in the bar cart, I know because I had just been there, and the bartender asked where the champagne was and if it was already chilled.

Turns out there was another kitchen, a mile and a half from the reception space, empty save for the champagne and some wine in boxes. Who was going to bring this all down? I thought it wouldn't be a bad idea if this particular stash were forgotten. Did I mention the bride and groom were supplying their own liquor to save on costs? A good idea, really. But this ultimately meant that 'no one owned the liquor.' Sure, on paper, the bartender should, or at the very least, the caterer, as they took care of all food and drink, but I could already see the writing on the wall. The caterer didn't want the responsibility. I had too much on my plate to handle this, too. But it would fall to me, as ultimately, all fell to me.

I found the warm champagne next to the industrial-sized fridge and grabbed two bottles. I'd have to beg a semi-sober groomsman to put the cases in the fridge to chill. They were too heavy for me to do so. I put that task on my mental checklist.

Back in my car, I drove the champagne down to the bride at the security cabin.

"What took you so long?" The bride snarled at me without thanks. She grabbed the two bottles roughly and wobbled off back to her photographer. She stumbled twice. Oh no. She was good and drunk. Her makeup was smeared. Should I tell her? No, I'd leave it to the professionals. I saw that her hair and makeup team's car was still in the parking lot.

All too soon, it was time to line up the bridal party for the procession. I was thankful to see that the father of the bride had taken a shower and changed out of his dirty biker-dude leathers. He wasn't sober, however. The groomsmen had cleaned up nicely, but one had trouble standing upright. I wasn't sure if I should recommend him stepping out. But feared the wrath of the groom, who seemed rather sober. He actually seemed like a nice guy; I felt sorry for him marrying this bride. I don't think she would make his life easy. He looked at me sadly, but I still didn't think he'd take kindly to me suggesting one of his bros stand out.

The mother of the bride, divorced from the father of the bride, swayed into my arms. I caught her, just in time. She laughed; I didn't. What a disaster. Had a wedding party ever been this 'off' before the wedding? Not one of my weddings.

Somehow, we got through the ceremony, on time! I think the justice of the peace was going to mince no words. We had had a little talk right before the ceremony. We agreed we needed to get this 'over with.'

The bride and groom made it to dinner. Thank God. I have never had to revive a wedding couple or make excuses for their absence. We got the buffet lined up and running…on time! While the guests were noshing, the vendors finally got a chance to have their meal. I was nauseous at this point and decided to skip it. I wandered around, making sure everything was progressing as it should. Then I heard it…the name 'Clyde.'

"I wonder what's going to happen to his clients who have outstanding wedding photos?" Said a woman in a shiny teal dress.

" Good question, Tina!" replied the woman to her right as she did her best to climb over the bolted-down bench with her modesty intact. No easy feat, as her dress, a very low-cut black affair, was quite short. She wobbled a little on her red stilettos but ultimately wiggled into her seat. I was impressed.

"Did you go to Hunter Riley's wedding?" Tina asked. "I heard he did her photos. I wonder if he was able to get them back to her before, you know…"

"Yes, why didn't I see you there?" Black Dress inquired. Wait…was she mad?

"Oh, Jeeze. Brandy had the flu. I was tempted to leave her with my mother-in-law, that old cow never gets sick, but Cole wouldn't let me. He worships that woman." Tina had a rather ugly look on her face. I feel pretty confident she was not a fan of her mother-in-law.

Black Dress seemed to relax. Wow, jealous much? "Hope she's feeling better," she replied. "The wedding was to die for, I bet it was a quarter of a million."

Wowzah! Wish I had been the planner for that shindig!

"Anyway, he did her wedding, and I bet the photos are gorgeous." Black Dress continued.

Hunter Riley, Hunter Riley. Where had I read or heard that name? I know I had recently. I was tired, but I knew it would come to me.

Chapter Five

The next day, I learned the devastating news that the police were focusing on Addalee Baker for the murder of Clyde Bunker; yes, my good friend, Addalee, who I have known since we were in elementary school. She was my high school buddy, and I had done her wedding last year.

Addalee had a rough start to her life. She grew up with an alcoholic father and a cowed mother. She was teased mercilessly until high school, when she grew into her beauty. Then she was frozen out by the jealous girls who thought it 'wasn't fair' that the fair-haired Cory was dating her. The magical two-some broke up for several years, but finally reunited three years ago, and it was my pleasure to plan their wedding. Addalee had confided in me last week that they were expecting their first child. She was the same age as I, thirty-eight. Yes, there was still time, I reminded myself. But did I want another child? I so enjoyed my career. I loved the freedom having an almost adult child gave me. Of course, there were different worries and concerns when one had a high schooler vs having a little one. I knew that. But I also loved Brian, and I felt that a baby was part of the package. Was that fair? I didn't know.

"Katie?" Addalee said. Oh dear, I had lost my thoughts.

"Sorry, Addie!" I looked at her guiltily. We were sitting at one of the café tables by the fountain. The fountain in the center of Main Street was more than just a little park where townsfolk could enjoy a cup of coffee or chat with a friend. It was the local spot where all the high schoolers met with their dates (and families!) to have their photos taken before Junior Prom and Senior Ball. Brides often had their 'First Look' with their grooms here, and often, it was the site for engagement photos and even baptism photos. It was all that and more.

The weather was mild for fall, with a gentle breeze ruffling our hair. It felt cool and soft on my neck. Even in her worry, Addalee was beautiful; sea green eyes, and pale, pale hair that one usually didn't see on a mature woman unless she visited her hairstylist monthly. Her skin was clear, and if I didn't know better, I'd think she also used Botox on a frequent basis. But not only did Addalee confide in me that she'd never do such a thing, as she was pregnant, but she moved her face with ease. I asked her once, around the time of her wedding, what her secret was.

She smiled and said, "Simple. Really, good genes, which you can't control, and stay out of the sun, which you can. Oh, and a good moisturizer." Then she complimented me, as her kindness demanded.

I gave myself a mental shake. Listen, Kate, I cautioned. Listen!

Addalee looked down at her hands holding her paper coffee cup as she spoke, and I had to lean in to hear her. "It was silly, really. I was Clyde's second shooter for the Ridgewood wedding, remember?" I did. It wasn't *my* wedding, but that of my rival, Ivy. Ivy was new to the game of wedding planning and was willing to set the bar extremely low on the price point. Fair enough, that's how I started out, but it still cut into my business. When I had to compete with her, it stung.

"Well, at the last minute, the bride decided she wanted a second shooter. I'm talking *last minute,* as in a day ahead of the wedding. Apparently, the bride had just had her Bachelorette Party, and her maid of honor had been married the month before. *She* had a second shooter. Ah, the peer pressure and the need to keep up 'with the Joneses.' A second shooter is exactly what it sounds like: a second photographer.

Addalee's thumbnail began to work the curled lip of the paper coffee cup.

"He chose me. Lucky me, I thought. I was so excited. You know how I've been trying to get my business up and running? Well, the day of the wedding, all was going fine. Then we had a terrible fight, and he accused me of being alone with the card box, right in front of the bride and bridesmaids. I was mortified, to put it mildly. We bickered, a big 'no, no' at an event, but I had to defend myself. I had to! Addalee was very emotional at this point. "I know it's not good to get defensive. But it was important to me that the bridesmaids heard me say, 'I didn't do it.' I finally pulled the plug and ended the verbal battle. So, let's just say, it was known by a lot of people that we weren't friends. Then there was the whole thing with Charlie and Remley."

I stopped my stupor of staring at Addalee's hands picking at her coffee cup, and my eyes shot up to hers. Those beautiful sea-green eyes were swimming with tears.

"Charlie and Remley?" I asked softly, a question in my voice. "But when they came to me, they said Clyde was their photographer. I momentarily wonder why they didn't pick you. You were long-time friends with Charlie and all. But just thought you'd want to be a guest, not a vendor at their wedding." I had seen Clyde's work, and it was sound, actually, really good. I didn't want to make Addalee feel any worse than she did by bragging on Clyde's talent, though.

Addalee stood and paced around the circular fountain. It was still bubbling in the fall breeze. It would be shut down for the winter soon, so the plumbing wouldn't freeze. But for now, we could enjoy its peaceful babble.

"Oh, Charlie and Remley asked me. And I was so excited. I do my best work when I know the couple, and we have made plans to pick a location for the engagement shoot. We would come here for sure, and maybe Cotton Hollow (the town's local Lovers' Lane). Then Remley called me and said how disappointed they were that I was already booked, and it was such poor form that I didn't have the professionalism to tell them myself. I was stunned. 'What?' Was all I could ask. Remley continued in that superior tone, telling me how Clyde had let them know and 'saved the day,' and stepped in to offer his services. I tried to defend myself, but Remley disconnected with the parting shot that they couldn't promise *not* to leave a negative review on my

Google page.

"Oh my gosh!" I reached out and pulled Addalee back down on the café chair next to me. "You called Charlie to clear it up, right? And I sure hope you gave Clyde a piece of your mind!"

A tear rolled down Addalee's cheek. She was not usually this emotional, but if she was anything like I had been when I was pregnant with Ellis, she was more emotional than usual.

"I got my nerve up and did call Charlie. But he was in court and never did return my call. I decided to let it go."

I was so irritated with Charlie. He knew Addalee wouldn't act this way professionally! And who was Clyde to him anyway? I felt confident that the lovely Remley had something to do with this debacle. Maybe she was jealous of Addalee and didn't want her man around her? More attractive women than Remley had reacted the same way.

"What about Clyde? Did you give him a piece of your mind?"

Addalee was quiet. I listened to the birds chirping and the cars driving by. The birds would soon be gone, flying south for the winter. I'd miss them.

"I did call him, told him I was letting it go, but it wasn't cool. I also told him not to call in a favor for me to be a second shooter for him again. He just laughed and said this wedding would fully put him on the map, and he didn't need me."

I didn't want to be harsh, but I wish Addie had fought back. She seemed to know what I was thinking, because she spun her engagement ring, a four-carat cushion cut in platinum—her nervous tic.

"I know I should have carried it through and kept trying to contact Charlie; we all go back a long way. But I just couldn't. Cory," her husband, "said to let it go. It's not like we need the money." She said almost in embarrassment. Cory's family was one of the biggest landowners in the area. Addalee kept her hand in photography for the love of the art, not as a way to earn an income. I understand why she wouldn't imply that Charlie had infringed on their friendship, but I hated to see her pushed around. I had seen too much of that in high school.

"Remley was just so mean, I didn't want to rock the boat. We know whose back Charlie would have, as he should." Addalee did an elegant shoulder shrug. "I let it go."

I took a sip of my now tepid coffee. "So, you let it go, it's over," I covered Addalee's hand with my own. "Stop worrying." I gave her hand a gentle squeeze.

"But that's just it, Katie, I can't. Brian came to see me at home today. And he had a lot of questions. Did you know Clyde was shot with an arrow?"

"I heard, Addie," And then Addalee's worry settled in my chest. Addalee was a winter Olympic hopeful in archery. **According to Wikipedia.org,**

"In Olympic archery, competitors use recurve bows that draw an average of 48.5 pounds for the men and 33 pounds for the women. The bow may have a mechanical sight, but no optical enhancements. It may also feature stabilizers on the bow."

Addalee was obviously skilled with a bow and arrow and had motive. But no one would believe she was a killer…would they?

All I could say was, "Oh crap, Addalee." Then I thought to add, "I'm sure you have an alibi?" I wonder if she heard the hope in my voice. She looked somewhere over my shoulder, not meeting my eyes.

"Cory will say anything I want him to; he'd vouch for me. But no, I don't have an alibi for Clyde's time of death. I know his time of death is sometime between 11:00 PM and midnight, because Brian asked me where I was then."

Chills ran down my spine. What in the heck? Where would pregnant Addalee be without Cory at midnight, *any* night?

Just ask her, my little inner voice said. "Where were you, Addie?'

This time, she did meet my eyes. And those amazing sea-green eyes implored me to believe her, to understand.

"Cory and I had a fight. It seems so stupid now, if I could go back and not get mad…" she trailed off and sat up straight. "We had a fight because his mother wants to be in the delivery room when the baby's born."

"What the heck? No, nope, no way. What is he *thinking*?" I was irate on her behalf.

"It's not Cory, it's his mother. She has her heart set on it. This baby will be her first grandchild, and she wants to hold him/her right away." Okay, we'll have to revisit this situation after this whole mess is straightened out. But WOW. Cory should have Addalee's back. He should support her and do whatever she wants in this situation.

"This is material for another conversation after we've cleared this… whatever this is…up." I grabbed her hand again. "Alibi?" I gently reminded her.

Addalee put a protective hand on her, as of now, still-flat stomach. "So, Cory and I had that fight about his mom, and I left the house, about 11:00. I took our dog, then walked in our neighborhood up and down the streets and cried. Then I asked myself why it bothered me so much. And if I'm going to be honest, it's because my own mom isn't here, and…the fact that Jilly has never liked me." Well, I knew that much to be true. Jilly, Cory's mom, did everything she could think of when we were in high school to break up Addalee and Cory. Didn't work then, but they did break up for a while after.

"Maybe someone saw you?" I asked hopefully.

Addalee looked almost annoyed. "And who would that be, Katie?"

Chapter Six

When planning your tablescape, think height, texture, and color. For height, you need some décor to be tall, and others short, as in different heights of candlesticks. For texture, envision lace or other textures to complement your plain tablecloths. For example, place an overlap of lace on top of your tablecloth. And color...use your wedding colors and employ items other than just flowers, such as colored glass.

Addalee left, worry on her pretty face, for her OB appointment. She did smile when she told me Cory would meet her there. They had had such a rough time getting together, I hoped the best for them. I told Addalee, in no uncertain terms, that she needed to consult an attorney, as the police had already reached out for an interview. She should have no more such meetings without representation. Would she take my advice? I had no way of knowing. I sure hope so, though.

I dropped into Jen's. I needed another coffee. No one was there I felt like chatting with. I saw a few familiar faces, but then I always did in our small town of Eastbury. Neither Jen nor her right-hand Tally was behind the bar. Dang it. I really wanted to get his worry over Addalee off my chest. What the heck?

I grabbed a chair, sat down, and pulled my phone out of my pocket. I fired off a text to Sarah:

Coffee? The bubbles were working.

Sure, came the reply. *Jen's?*

Yep.

See you in 5

Sarah arrived in three minutes—just long enough for me to get us each a cup of black coffee. We didn't have time for any specialty drinks right now. Sarah looked gorgeous as usual. Today she was dressed in black silk pants, wide and billowy, (I could never wear those, I'd look like a clown in them. But Sarah was tall and very thin; it worked), and a lilac silk blouse. She carried what I speculated was a green Hermes Kelly bag, but I wasn't sure. I sure wasn't going to ask her. She'd *love* to tell me all about it. There were so many knockoffs these days, who knows?

"What's up, Manet?" She pulled out the chair across from me and slid in.

"Thanks for the coffee."

"No time for small talk, Sarah. I just had coffee with Addalee."

"And this is important to me because…"

I gave Sarah the stink eye. "Let's put the snark aside, Sarah, this is important."

Sarah frowned. While we had not been friends in high school, Sarah had never been a bully. I remember more than one time when she had stood up for Addalee. I knew that they had remained friends of a sort ever since.

"Okay…" she said, looking worried. I knew Sarah better now, and knew she was a softie when it came to her friends. "Is everything okay with the baby?"

I was surprised. "She told you about the baby?"

"Of course, she told me, Katie. We're friends. Jeeze. You don't have a monopoly on old high school buddies here in good ol' Eastbury." Now she looked annoyed, one fine frown line was popping out on her forehead right between her eyes. I liked that imperfection.

"She and the baby are fine, physically.

"Physically…" Sarah seemed to draw out the word, and her face drooped. "But something else is wrong? This can't be good for her."

I almost wanted to cover her hand with mine as I had Addalee's, but…no.

"Well, as you know, Clyde was shot with an arrow."

"So? I'm pretty sure I told *you* about that." Sarah was all about the snark again; she didn't like anyone to see her vulnerable side, especially me.

I ignored her. "Addalee told me today that she and Clyde had worked a wedding together, and he embarrassed her in public. Bad blood there. Then, Charlie asked Addalee to photograph his and Remley's wedding. A few days after…Remley called Addalee and said she was sorry that Addalee was booked for another wedding, but she really should have told them up front. But, never fear, Clyde let them know, and he was available for their wedding. Addalee was gutted and mad, but you know Addie. She just let it go."

Sarah shook her head in gentle upset, her double pearl drops swinging gently. I love that style. I just may have to get a copy of the pair. "That girl. I don't know what to do to get her some backbone. So, what's the fallout?"

"Brian made her a visit and asked, in so many words, for an alibi."

Sarah pursed her lips in a contemplative mode. She tapped a pink lacquered nail on the scarred tabletop. "And I'm guessing she has no alibi?"

"Nope."

Sarah stood, gulped her black coffee down, grimaced, made a face, then said, "Next time, if you want to remain my friend, order me an oat milk vanilla latte with just a dash of nutmeg. If this alibi thing becomes an issue, we'll revisit and fix it." She cocked a brow at me. "Keep me posted. And she was off in a cloud of Chanel no.19.

Well, Sarah was on board, as I knew she would be. Now, what could I do in the meantime? I'd investigate Clyde, is what I'd do. No better place to start than a quick internet dive. It was not hard on the internet. As a wedding vendor, he would need to have a significant online presence. I took the inner staircase up to my office. I liked to use the inner entrance during my business hours, especially in inclement weather. I ran up the stairs two at a time. Take that, bum leg, I said to myself. I shivered when I thought of my broken femur. How I hated that long road of rehab, but how I loved wearing skirts and dresses again. I recognized that I was still very self-conscious of the nasty scar on my leg.

I unlocked my door quickly and entered my paradise.

I tossed my Louis Vuitton Never Full (by the way, not a knock off—it was purchased when we lived in California and were flush with money—today,

I'd never think of spending the ridiculous amount), and sank into my desk chair. It was okay comfort-wise, but not great. Luckily, I never spent that much time sitting. I really needed to do more, so much more, admin work for those pesky weddings. I dreamt of the day when I could hire someone to take care of the mundane tasks.

I fired up my trusty Apple AirBook and went right to theknot.com, the premier wedding website for wedding planning. I searched photographers and found Clyde. I wondered if he had anyone who would deactivate his account and contact pending weddings of his passing. I realized how little I knew of the man. He had some good reviews, and one "one-star" review, which meant nothing, as I knew from the recent nasty bride. She had contacted me yesterday via email and told me that if I didn't refund all her money, she'd write me a one-star review. Can you say 'extortion'? I said no and she wrote the one-star review. Hateful. I now read Clyde's reviews:

"Clyde's work is *amazing*, but he has a dark side. He was moody and angry on my day. He was constantly on his cell and appeared to be arguing with someone on a call during my wedding. It did not make me feel good. That being said, my photos were beautiful. Was he worth it? I'm not sure. He is super expensive."

This didn't surprise me, given what Addalee had shared. But helpful it wasn't. I went to Google reviews. He came right up, and this time there weren't as many favorable reviews. More of the same, *"Clyde was in a bad mood, on his phone, but his work was really good."*

But the next post stood out because someone responded to more of the same negative words with a blast of his/her own.

"Clyde is amazing. He works so hard. He's a true artist. You people just don't get his magic. Leave him alone!" It was signed by **@sylvie123**. Of course, there was no picture. So, who was **@sylvie123**?

I went to Clyde's Instagram. His photos were beautiful. They were dark and brooding, not my personal preference for wedding pictures, but it was what some people were looking for. So, was **@sylvie123** an Instagram follower? Dollars to donuts she was. I searched his followers in the "S's" and found her. I clicked on her name. Private, darn it all. The profile picture was of a hot pink flower, a peony. Not much help. LinkedIn? I exited Instagram and went to my LinkedIn page. Ah, my account needed work. I had such a hard time keeping up with all the social media platforms. I doubted many potential clients looked for a wedding planner on LinkedIn, however. I went to Clyde's account and then his followers. He had several "Sylvias" in his connections. High school principal, real estate agent, attorney, and…a kindergarten teacher. And this particular kindergarten teacher had the same last name as Clyde, a sister? That was my bet. I clicked on her account. She was a new teacher, based on her length of time at her current school, year of college graduation, and…her photo. Wow. Had I ever been that young? She had a phone number attached to her contact info, bingo. I had a way to contact **@sylvie123**, who I felt sure was Clyde's sister. But if she *was* his sister, she would be grieving. I'd have to think of a way to approach her in a respectful manner. This was hard! And know what else was hard? I had to figure out what was for dinner tonight. I never knew how Ellis would be feeling. Some days, she was ravenous; others, she ate like a bird. I think she was hungrier on the days she didn't have a scheduled lunch break. I packed her a lunch regardless of her schedule, but I doubled up the days she had no formal lunch period. I had been hesitant to agree to her taking an additional class, AP French, during the only period she could fit in lunch Mondays, Wednesdays, and Fridays, but she pushed. And so did her darn father. Grant had his heart set on Ellis getting as much scholastic financial aid as possible. She would need that GPA high to do so. AP courses sure helped. She seemed happy and was more than keeping up with Volleyball and her studies. But I was keeping my eye on the situation.

A stop at Whole Foods was in order, especially as I had a wedding rehearsal later tonight. I used to make Stop and Shop my 'go to,' but they had made the checkout process so difficult, I found myself more and more at Whole Foods. Today, I headed to the pre-packaged meals. I picked a walnut strawberry salad for me, and a pesto salad for Ellis. I picked up a bag of oranges and a few bagels for breakfast and headed to the self-check lane. A young woman exited the self-check pod, and she looked amazingly like **@sylvie123**, but I'm afraid it was wishful thinking. But it got me thinking. Maybe she shopped here? Maybe she stopped off after work. I would have to check out Stop and Shop, too. Where else would she go? How else could I contact her? Could I just go to the local elementary? But how well would that go? I have no reason to be there. My daughter was in high school. And then it occurred to me. Ellis needed volunteer hours. What better way to get them than reading to kindergarten students? I almost ran to my Suburban and raced home.

Ellis and I arrived about the same time. Today, she was driving the two-year-old Subaru Outback that Grant had gifted her for her birthday. I worried when she was out in it, I worried when she was with friends in their cars, I worried when she was being chauffeured by her boyfriend. Is the picture clear? I worried about her in a car all the time. But boy, did that car make my life easier. And even though we had not gotten to the level where she was driving in the snow, I loved that the Outback was all-wheel drive.

I grabbed my Whole Foods bags and trotted into the house. Both of us had to park in the driveway. Yes, we had a garage, but it was a former carriage house and a separate structure. We stored all our junk in there. Someday soon, I'd get it cleaned out and replace the doors with something user-friendly. But for now, we would both have to deal with scraping snow off our cars in the winter.

Ellis was in the mudroom removing her sneakers. She was lovely. Taller than I at five-foot-nine, she was a willowy beauty generally only seen in a teen woman. Her hair was the same rich chestnut as mine, her eyes my blue.

"Hey, Mom," she smiled. Oh, it was going to be a good night.

I smiled back. "Hey, Honey. How was your day?" My little dachshund, Chloe, came running to meet me. Ellis must have just taken her out. I gave her a pat, more later, but I had other fish to fry.

"Good, Mom. How was yours?"

"Not bad. I got Whole Foods," I held up my prize.

"Please tell me you got me the pesto." She looked at me with hope in her eyes.

This was going to be too easy. "You bet ya."

Soon, we were sitting at the kitchen table, eating our dinner. Now was the time. "So, Elle, how's the count going for your community service hours?"

Her fork stopped midway to her mouth. "Uugggg. Not well. There's just no time."

"I know. But you have to get at least ten hours this semester for the National Honor Society. I was thinking—how about reading to some elementary school children? I heard they're always looking for readers." I coyly looked down at my salad. Best not to look her in the eye. She'd see through me if I did.

I glanced up. She was looking to the right, thinking. "When would I do this? It would have to be during the day."

"I know. The elementary school starts before you do, so maybe before you go to school?"

"I think that would be fun." Ellis agreed. Wait, this was too easy.

"Okay, want some help setting it up?" I calmly queried. This could be tricky; she could be so independent. A pause and then…

A smile. "That would be great, Mom. Thanks." Chloe jumped on my leg. To celebrate my success, I snuck her a piece of lettuce. The dog loved lettuce. Weird, I know.

Chapter Seven

Give some thought to the added expense and time to steam your tablecloths. Whatever your reservations, it's worth it. Your guests won't notice if they are wrinkle free, but they will notice if they are not.

Tonight, I had a rehearsal for a wedding tomorrow at one of my favorite venues, Branford House in Groton, Connecticut. **According to Wikipedia:**

*The **Branford House** is located in Groton, Connecticut, on the campus of UConn Avery Point, which rents it out for events. Branford House was built in 1902 for Morton Freeman Plant, a local financier and philanthropist, as his summer home; he named it after his hometown of Branford, Connecticut. The house was added to the National Register of Historic Places on January 23, 1984.*

When built in 1902, Branford Manor cost $3 million—an incredible sum of money at the time. Plant shunned the high society of Newport and chose instead the wide views of Long Island Sound available at Avery Point.

Branford House was designed by Plant's wife, Nellie (who had a Sorbonne education in architecture), and built by Robert W. Gibson. Although the outside was built to the Tudor style to match the estate, the interior was a patchwork of various styles—"Gothic, Baroque, Renaissance, Classical, and even Flemish"—desired by the Plants. The house included a two-story fireplace surrounded by a clothes-drying conveyor belt, a then-rare elevator, and other architectural curiosities like doors leading into exterior walls.

Plant fancied himself a 'gentleman farmer' and built vast agricultural facilities on the grounds. These included huge greenhouses (including one to store his tropical plants during the winter), a 22,250-square-foot (2,067 m²) cow barn, poultry enclosures, and fruit and vegetable fields. The estate totaled more than 70 acres (0.28 km²), including carpentry and plumbing shops, a boarding house, and other buildings. Bothered by its smell, Plant bought the Quinnipiac Fertilizer Company on nearby Pine Island and replaced it with an orchard where his grandchildren played.

In 1967, the property was transferred back to the state for use as a satellite campus of the University of Connecticut, though the buildings were largely in poor condition. By the 1980s, the house needed millions of dollars of renovations, which UConn could not afford; there was discussion of a private developer turning it into a conference center, or of the town taking over the property. The building was added to the National Register of Historic Places on January 23, 1984.

Ultimately, UConn carried out renovations to the house, which were completed in 2001. The house is not in regular academic use; UConn rents it out for event uses. The second floor of the Branford House is home to the Alexey von Schlippe Gallery of Art.

* * *

The ceremony was going to be out on the lawn. Fall in New England was fairly rain-free, but it just may snow. One never knew. We were lucking out with as perfect weather as we could hope for in early October—a high of seventy-two degrees. It was always windy here on the Sound, though, and today was no exception. I was worried about the wooden arch that the family was going to set up, and the florist would decorate it tomorrow. It was going to be a thing of beauty with five hundred blooms and lots of greenery. Had the family remembered to bring tent stakes? The father of the bride had assured me he would stop by Lowe's and get some, but did he? I'd ask him tonight.

"Kate!" Everly, my bride, came running toward me and threw herself into my arms. She was a 'cute as a button' redhead and very coltish in appearance. Her freckles seemed to glow with health and happiness. Her busy mane of hair was pulled into a no-nonsense ponytail, but I knew it would be coiffed into an elaborate updo tomorrow. Everly had shown me pictures of her trial do, and it was gorgeous.

"I'm so excited, I can hardly stand it!" Everly said as Ben, her groom, came ambling toward us and gave me a chaste kiss on the cheek.

"Big day tomorrow," he deadpanned. I smiled at him. He was an absolute gem. Then the rub of the whole day approached, the Matron of Honor, Hunter. Oh my gosh! My eyes widened. That's where I knew the name 'Hunter' from! The guest from last night's wedding mentioned "Hunter's wedding" and the fact that Clyde had been the photographer. The Matron of Honor, 'MOH,' was a piece of work. That must be why I blanked on the name. I wished to forget her. There should be a term coined for Maid-zillas. She was about the best I have ever seen. She thought she could do everything I did, only better, as she had recently gotten married. I pasted a smile on my face to greet her as warmly as possible. It wouldn't help me to make an enemy at this late hour. I think she felt the same way, because she gave me the first genuine smile I'd seen on her face. Now I remembered that I *had* seen her wedding photos. What a golden opportunity. Women love to talk about two things, always, their weddings and their birth stories.

I intercepted Hunter and led her a little bit toward the arch. "Hunter, I want your opinion on the sturdiness of the arch." I oozed. No question, her grin was real this time. Who doesn't like to be asked their opinion?

Hunter walked with purpose toward the arch. "I know! I woke up last night worrying about it. It really needs some tent stakes with this perpetual wind." Wait, what? This girl may just be too good to be true. I took my jealousy blinders off.

I looked at Hunter square on. "Hunter, do you want a job?" She turned toward me and blushed.

"I thought you'd never ask. I've been doing my utmost to impress you. I loved doing my own wedding and just don't want to leave this world. So yeah, I'd love a job." And we both laughed. This could be wonderful. I knew Hunter's new husband was soon to be a partner in his father's law firm, so she didn't have to work, unless she wanted to. I imagine when they had kids, she would be a 'stay at home,' but for now, I could pass on to her all my weddings I had to say 'no' to because I was already booked. I'd plan them, and she'd be the 'day of.' Maybe I'd hire more ladies…okay, Kate, get a grip. Focus.

"What are you doing Monday morning? Can we chat? I think this will be a good fit." She hugged me with such enthusiasm we almost toppled over on the uneven lawn. I'd wait to ask her about Clyde until then. I was happy to see that the father of the bride had done his job and secured the arch with those tent stakes. So far, so good.

Chapter Eight

Consider a late-night snack for your guests. Sometimes, when there is an open bar, guests indulge more than planned. And if you do have an open bar, think long and hard about a bus for your guests. If you can afford it, it's a good choice. Safety first!

Everly's wedding on Saturday was a rocking success. She had a mariachi band for Cocktail Hour, and it got the party jumping. It wasn't a hard thing to do. The guests were mainly young and happy to be there. Most of them were from California, where Everly and her new husband now resided, and they were excited to be experiencing New England. Everly made sure there was some classic New England fare, including lobster rolls, and clam chowder. The day didn't disappoint either, with temperate weather and a spectacular sunset. The California kids flocked to get their photos taken with the orange and red magic.

* * *

On Sunday morning, I was sitting in the bleachers at Eastbury High School getting ready to watch Ellis and her team face the undefeated St. Carmel's girls' volleyball team. We usually didn't have games on Sunday, but it had to be rescheduled due to the St. Carmel bus breaking down on a previously scheduled game day.

Ellis was a junior this year and had earned a starting position on the team. It didn't hurt that she had my ex, Grant's, height. She was a gifted softball player, but not at the same level as a volleyball player. She had to fight in every game to keep her starting position.

The gym looked like something out of the fifties, all wooden walls and ceilings–but I wasn't fooled by the aesthetics. It was state-of-the-art, from the bleachers to the gym floor. The Town of Eastbury, Connecticut, did an outstanding job of keeping the 'village vibe' thing going, while still updating the town's infrastructure. Take the high school's science wing. We had recently done a renovation of it, as well as the gym and pool, to the tune of sixty million. Many of the older folks in town were dead set against it. I get it. If your children are grown, you personally don't want to invest in a building you'll never get any use out of. But maybe their grandchildren will? Eastbury has a very low rate of its citizens relocating after high school graduation. Back to the science wing, it rivaled many small colleges' labs. I don't think Ellis and her friends knew how lucky they were.

My mom trudged up the bleachers to the top to join me. She and my dad tried to make every one of Ellis' events.

I loved my mom. She was in many ways my best friend. She loved me unconditionally, the way only a mother can. "Hey, Mom!" I greeted her with my best smile. Want me to move down some?" I hated to see her climb; I knew her knees ached.

"I'm fine," she panted, only slightly. "Your father sends his regards. He has a nasty cold coming on, and we both thought it would be best for him to stay home and rest." My parents didn't make a decision without consulting each other. When it was election time, they read each proposal together and discussed each candidate—although they always voted along party lines. Something the debate on those proposals got heated, but they always compromised and decided together. I admired them and hoped I could have that type of relationship someday. Still amazes me that I ended up with old Grant as my husband.

Mom looked a lot like me. Or should I say I looked a lot like my mother? With the exception of those aging knees, my mom felt and looked remarkable. Her skin was amazing, and she was slim and fit. I know she walked a couple of miles every day. She dyed her hair her original brown to match her eyes, but she had confided in me that she was close to letting it go its natural gray. Would she? I didn't think she would for a while.

"I saw Brian at the dry cleaner." Mom shared, looking out at the volleyball court. The first game had started, and Ellis was serving. Ace! They didn't return her first serve, but the opponents broke her next serve.

Now, why was Mom mentioning seeing Brian at the dry cleaners? "Nice?" I asked with a question in my voice.

"He was very...agitated." My mom still didn't look at me. My mother was very neutral about my relationship with Brian. She never said anything negative, but she wasn't joyful about it either.

Alarm bells went off. "What do you mean, agitated, Mom?" Was Brian's temper getting the better of him again?

"I walked into the cleaners after Brian, and he didn't see me. It appeared that he had been in a dispute over a missing suit. They had lost it, or at least he accused them of losing it. He was..."

I gave Mom the 'come on' motion with my hand. "He was what, Mom?

Mom looked down at her hands. "Well, almost belligerent. He just wouldn't let it go. He was so angry."

This caused me all sorts of anxiety. What was going on with Brian? I thought it curious, though, that he had two mishaps in the same week. First, the 'lost' reservation, now the lost suit at the cleaners. What was going on? I shrugged it off and turned my attention to the game.

Chapter Nine

Make sure the volume of your dancing music is at a volume that is comfortable for all your guests. It's never fun to have to shout when trying to communicate with friends and family. Your entertainment may brace against lowering the volume—for some reason, they love it very loud—but remember they work for you.

Very early Monday morning found me at Jen's, waiting for Hunter to talk about the job as my assistant (after this meeting, I was going to get Ellis settled in as a reader at the elementary school). I was fifteen minutes early, and Hunter may not know it, but she was taking her first test. Would she be early, on time, or late?

Five minutes later, Hunter walked in, her eyes scanning the room for me. She was ten minutes early. Phew.

"Sorry, Kate, I thought I'd beat you. I know how important it is to be early." Test one, check. Test two, check also. She was dressed professionally in a navy corduroy shirt dress and cute little black booties. As a business owner in the community, I never went out without professional attire...okay, I tried not to, ha ha. Today I was dressed in my usual khakis and twin sweater set, this time in pale pink. I had on my favorite pair of penny loafers and, of course, my favorite pearls, black today, both around my neck and in my ears.

"Love your pearls, Kate." I liked this girl.

"Thank you, Hunter. Now, before we get started, I wanted to say I'm sorry for the loss of your photographer, Clyde. I'm sure you got close working with him on your engagement and wedding photos."

Real tears filled Hunter's eyes, and her nose turned pink. She was fair in a non-descript type of way with ash blond hair. I think it just may be her natural color and hazel eyes. She was slim, but not skinny.

"I was gutted. He was a hot and cold type guy, but really cared about his work. He wanted the best for us and would take photos over and over to get what he considered the right shot. That was a little much, even for me," she almost chuckled, then thought better of it.

"I don't mean to sound insensitive, but did his murder surprise you?" I asked, then realized how silly that sounded, so I tried to reword it. "I mean…"

"I know what you mean. Sometimes when someone meets with a violent end, you're just not…shocked.

"Exactly," and well said. "Did he ever say anything that would lead you to believe he had any enemies?" I was blowing this; I was trying not to sound creepy or arouse suspicion. Someone behind the coffee bar dropped what sounded like a pile of plates. Ouch! But the distraction eased the awkwardness of this line of conversation.

"Yikes," Hunter said, turning around. But she didn't forget our thread. "There was one weird thing. We were doing our engagement shoot, and Clyde got a call. He looked at the phone, which he usually did if he got a call when we were shooting, but this time he frowned and said, 'I've got to take this.' He walked a few feet away, and I couldn't catch everything he was saying, You must think I'm terrible, Kate, eavesdropping like that." She looked down at her hands, and the blush came back.

"No, no," I was quick to assure her. "Go on."

"Well, I could tell he was arguing with someone, but toward the end of the call, he looked, well, scared. He finished the shoot and then wasn't interested in 'getting the perfect shot' anymore." Hunter continued.

Wow, Clyde was a very complicated person, and he sure didn't seem like a happy one.

Chapter Ten

If you have an open bar, have a last call about thirty minutes before the end of the evening. This is a gracious reminder to the guests that the event is ending soon, as well as a time for guests to have a glass of water or coffee before heading out.

After my *very* early morning coffee with Hunter, I headed over to the elementary school with Ellis.

We pushed the intercom to be let into the main office of Eastbury Elementary and were immediately granted access. We walked in the door and then into a mini vestibule before opening the last set of doors. The vestibule was supposed to help insulate the building in the winter months. I'm sure it helped. The constant opening and closing of doors and letting in frigid winter air would wreak havoc on oil heating bills!

We followed the directional sign to the main office building. School offices are organized with a great respect for hierarchy. The closer your desk is to the entry door, the lower status you have. The desk farthest from the door is for the 'School Secretary.' Always a woman, she wielded great power. We were to deal with an 'assistant.'

"Hello," I smiled. A smile can go a long way. "I'm Kate Ludlow, and this is my daughter, Ellis. We're here so Ellis can volunteer in Miss Bunker's kindergarten class.

A big smile back. "Welcome, Kate, Ellis," said the short, curvy assistant. She had shoulder-length frosted 'mom' hair styled in a kind of helmet. It was heavily gelled and hairsprayed within an inch of its life. She stood up and baby-stepped over to the long counter that divided the secretaries from the natives, pulling her blue cotton Henley shirt down as she did.

"I have your paperwork right here, Ellis. You're not eighteen yet, right?"

Ellis shook her head. "Not yet," she said softly.

"So, Mom," I hated when I was referred to as 'Mom' by strangers. I had just introduced myself as 'Kate.' "You'll need to sign these two forms, and Ellis here will be just in time for story hour before the littles go off for their gym class."

I read all the small print. As far as I was concerned, the Eastbury School District was a little too invasive. Everything is done online now; all forms have to be e-signed with no opportunity to add a special note or change what is already on the form. Case in point, when I filled out Ellis' emergency information, I had to agree that in order for the school to call 911 services in case of an emergency, I had to e-sign that the school district would have complete access at any time to Ellis' health records. Ah...no. When I called to ask how to agree to 911 without agreeing to allowing them access to her health records, they said they didn't know how to do it, as no one had ever questioned the form before. Really? We finally decided that they could print the form, and I'd sign it, while crossing out the clause allowing them access to her health record. I know for a fact they would not delay calling an ambulance in order to see if I had agreed to the call.

All seemed in order. I signed the permission slip, we said thank you, then listened to the secretary's directions to Sylvie's classroom. It was surprisingly easy to get her registered as a reading volunteer at Eastbury Elementary in Sylvie's kindergarten class. I tried not to feel as if I was using my child. Ellis *did* need those volunteer hours, and I needed to help Addalee.

The best thing about this whole mash-up was that I had a legit reason for being with Ellis, as she was a minor. Can you say, 'Perfect?'

We walked down the hall together in the direction of the kindergarten room, and I was feeling great about my plan.

Upon arriving at the kindergarten door, I said, "Hey, Ellis, since you're not around little kids much, how about I come in and say 'Hi' with you?" I was met with a death stare.

"Ah, hard no, Mom," She wasn't cracking a smile." She carried the two books she had brought with her, and entered the room…alone, closing the door almost in my face. Was I surprised?

"Sure, El," I said to the closed door.

I looked in the little skinny rectangular window in the door at the kindergarten room full of bright colors, light, and joy. I can't imagine a child not being thrilled to walk into that haven every morning. @Sylvie123, AKA 'Miss Bunker,' was a diminutive figure with a mop of brown curls, big brown eyes, and apple cheeks. When Ellis entered the classroom, she stopped addressing the children, put a finger to her lips, and all the students were instantly silent. I was impressed.

"Boys and Girls!" I could make out from my spot at the window, "I have the best surprise for you! We have a special guest today, Ms. Ludlow." She meant Ellis.

The children, as a group, clapped politely.

If I stood here much longer, I'd be asked to leave. School staff didn't take kindly to stalkers looking through classroom windows. I looked around in the hallway and saw a grouping of chairs. I balanced my larger than a six-year-old's bum on an impossibly small chair and again admired the beautiful hallway bulletin boards. Okay, so I hopped over to the door again and looked in the window. I was nervous for Ellis. Inside the classroom, the children sat in a circle on the bright, primary colored rug that I felt sure had been supplied by Sylvie. Those little extras almost always come out of the teachers' pockets. The children were listening politely to my Ellis read "If You Give a Mouse a Cookie." Ellis read two more books (the kids begged that she read a book from their own library). The class politely clapped after each book. Oh, they were darling. This made me realize how much I loved little kids. How could I deny Brian this joy, or myself? I sat back down in the tiny hallway chair again. I was nervous. Would I get a chance to ask Miss Sylvie Bunker a few questions? My plan was close to falling apart.

"Mom," I felt Ellis' hand on my shoulder. Where had I been? Deep in thought, I told myself.

"Rose, you know from the softball team?" I nodded. "Well, she just did some volunteer work here, too, and is heading to school. Okay if I catch a ride with her?" I smiled, what I hoped was a benign smile, when inside I was ready to burst. YES! Maybe I could get a chance to grill, I mean, gently question Miss Sylvie Bunker after all.

"Sure, Ellis, and thank Rose for me. You did a great job reading today, by the way."

"Thanks, Mom." But then she quirked an eye at me. "How would you know?" But Ellis dropped it, gave me a running kiss on the cheek (nice!), and was on her way.

"Children," Sylvie opened her classroom door and said gently to the class, "time to line up for gym class. We have a special treat; you are going to go outside today with Mr. Foster, so he will be here at any minute to pick you up. I'm glad to see that you all remembered to wear your gym shoes to class. Good job!" She looked so happy and proud of this simple feat, and the children's faces reflected that pride. Oh, she was one of the good ones. A teacher, Mr. Foster, I imagine, came into the hall and greeted the class. The kindergarteners followed his lead, their line straight as a pin. That was a feat in itself.

After the last little ones marched away, Sylvie turned her laser focus on me. Why did I all of a sudden feel super guilty? Oh yes, she was the best of the best. Only the best could make you feel guilty with a look.

"Ms. Ludlow?" I nodded. "How about a cup of coffee, Ms. Ludlow?" Music to my ears on more than one front.

"I would love that." My eyes met her pretty brown ones, and I followed her into her classroom.

"Let's go over to the 'adult space,' she indicated the right corner of the room by the windows that housed her desk and a pair of rocking chairs. On a long, low table behind the rockers was a Keurig machine with a plentiful assortment of coffee and tea pods. There was also an insulated mini thermos in which I could only hope was cream. There was also a sugar pot, honey packets, and bright colored cappuccino mugs—the perfect size for a quick pick-me-up. Oh, she was my kind of gal.

After I selected my brew, we settled into the rockers. "I just adore when the kids have specials." She was referring to the special programs led by the art, language, physical ed, librarians, and music teachers. These folks were heroes to both the overworked teachers and students alike.

We began to rock…and rock. I wasn't going to break the silence. Let's see how good she was. Yep, I was better, because she was the first to break the silence.

"Something on your mind, Ms. Ludlow?" She turned then, in her chair, and met my gaze head-on.

"I don't mean to make this awkward, but I was a casual business acquaintance of Clyde's, and I wanted to say how very sorry I am." I don't know why, but my eyes suddenly filled. Maybe because hers did.

Then she broke down. She grabbed a box of, I'm sure a very well-used box of tissues, and grabbed four in quick succession.

"I'm so sorry!" She whimpered behind her tissues and eventually blew her nose. "I haven't cried yet. I don't know why, and I don't know why I would with you, Ms. Ludlow."

"Kate, please. I'm sure we're on a first-name basis, now, right?" I gently squeezed the hand that wasn't actively wiping her nose.

'Kate," she smiled a watery smile. "He wasn't perfect, but he *was* my brother."

I squeezed her hand again. "No one's perfect.

"But who would want to kill him?" Sylvie put the wad of tissues to her mouth and cried silent tears of anguish. What had I done? I never meant to hurt her, to make her sad.

She seemed to pull herself together. "I'm good," and she did seem to gather her emotions. "Whew. I needed that. Glad I didn't let loose when the kids were here." She sniffed loudly.

Could I do this? Yeah, yeah, I could. "Did Clyde, did he have…" I stopped I don't think I could be that invasive to this poor young woman.

But she finished for me "Enemies? Probably a few. He dated Maria Di'Rissi on and off for several years. They had finally called it quits, and it didn't end well."

I had been gone a long time, but even I knew that name, that family. This put a whole new spin on the situation. I wonder if Brian knew about this.

"Had anything happened recently between them, any new bad blood?"

Sylvie rocked a few beats. "I'm not sure, but I do know they had been talking recently, and she wanted him to be her guest at a family wedding. He had mixed emotions about it; one, he was worried she would read too much into the wedding date, and he wasn't sure he wanted to get back together. Plus, I think there was someone new in his life. Additionally, her family never liked him, and frankly, he finally realized the whole situation was toxic, which I had been telling him for years." A bell sounded. "Yikes, first lunch already. The second graders have to eat so early to accommodate all our students."

I could read a room. It was time to take my leave. I stood up and so did Sylvie. Impulsively, I hugged her. And she hugged me back. She was a great hugger. I guess you have to be in order to be a good kindergarten teacher.

Chapter Eleven

Your wedding planner should not be in charge of your guest table assignments. You and your fiancé know your guest list best. Perhaps both of your parents can aid in the assignments if their friends are included?

I left the school happy that I had gleaned some information from Sylvie, and sad that I had made her cry. Perhaps it was therapeutic? 'Keep telling yourself that, Kate,' I scolded myself. The Di' Russi family, oh boy, nothing says mob family like 'Di' Russi.' The grandfather, Joseph Di 'Russi, had made his money in olive oil, and everything in between from drugs, prostitution, and guns. He had no moral code, no illegal area he would steer clear of. If it was cash-rich, he was in. He ruled the family, and his soldiers, with an iron fist. His son and heir, Ant (short for Anthony), was lazy, but had a brutal heart. What he didn't have in work ethic, he made up for in showing everyone who was boss. Maria was Ant's daughter. I can't imagine a man leaving Ant's beloved Maria unless he wanted him to. I almost felt sorry for Clyde. But the arrow, that was a weird mob hit, if it was one. But what did I know about mob hits? Only what I see on TV, and to be perfectly honest, that wasn't my kind of genre. If anyone knew about the mob, it was…Sarah Deloro. I'd have to check in.

* * *

"Katie, Katie, Katie," Sarah said as she prepared to take a sip of her caramel macchiato. We were once again at Jen's. "Just because we've had a bit of

fun these last few months doesn't mean we can be hanging out all the time."
Rude!

Today Sarah was dressed in Sarah casual—ironed dress jeans, a cream silk blouse paired with a taupe cashmere ribbed sweater, and soft as butter nude flats. She had the most gorgeous strand of black pearls I'd ever seen. She tipped her head just so as she looked at me, making the matching black pearl drop earrings bobble just so. I hated her.

Sarah met my glare with her own. "Sorry, Katie. The doc and I had a fight, and I'm in a crap mood about it." She looked deeply into her coffee. Was Sarah Deloro going to…cry? She had just started dating the dreamy cardiologist, and I think she really had feelings for him. Those first fights were devastating. Heck, all the fights Brian and I had lately *were* devastating.

"Dang, Sarah, that sucks." She seemed to be comforted by my simple words.

"Okay, Manet, what's up? Why the early rally call? And by the way, what are you doing after this little 'Meet and Greet'? Cause if that's what you wear out and about as a local business owner, we have work to do." Sarah did a quick sweeping gaze down my outfit. She didn't look impressed.

I too looked down at my outfit of the day, a pair of khakis, my standard sweater set, yellow today, and my very plain *white* pearls. "Hey," I was ready to go to the mat with Sarah over this, then she laughed.

"The…look…on…your…face, Katie," Sarah wheezed in between bursts of laughter. I feel better already." Then she was straight-faced. "But seriously, we need to go shopping soon. You've done some real body firming, and you need to show it off. And you're not doing yourself any favors in," and here she waved my hand all over my being, "that."

I don't think she was trying to be mean, and if I were honest with myself, it wouldn't hurt to do a little shopping therapy. Sarah was correct. I had been working on my health, and a wonderful side effect, in addition to the weight loss, was that I was stronger, firmer. Might as well show it off. Wow, did I really just think that? Yuck. Sarah was wearing off on me.

"Fiiiiinnneee." I sounded like Ellis. "Let's do the shopping thing, but not today. Tell me, here I leaned toward Sarah, "about the Di'Rissi family. I know you have listed, sold, helped buy homes for them."

The playful smile on Sarah's face disappeared. "You know I can't talk about any of my clients, Katie." She was all serious now, and did she look a little...scared?

"I know, Sarah, I don't want any personal information or financials, just a general...feeling?" I decided not to mention the fact that she had been very generous in discussing Charlie's financials.

"No can do, Katie. They're too big a fish, too powerful. I just can't go there."

She pushed her chair away from the table, and it scraped jarringly on the bare floor, hurting my ears and those of folks around us. "And I have one of the daughters' weddings this weekend."

The minute she said it, we both knew what was going to happen. She froze. I know she was mentally kicking herself. I smiled at her. She didn't smile back. Was that sweat breaking out on her upper lip? I had to play this with finesse.

"Sarah..." I wheedled.

Sarah scooted her chair in, leaned her arms on the table toward me. "No, Katie."

"You know you owe me for throwing me under the bus last spring with our mutual client. That wasn't...nice." I cocked an eyebrow at her.

"Oh my God! You are never going to let this go, are you? She hissed, "I was mad, okay? What I did was petty. I have apologized, and I thought you accepted. And nothing detrimental happened. Your business is intact, no harm, no foul." Her face fell. "You're not going to give in on this, are you? You're going to torment me until I give in?" Then she got a cagey look in her eye. I didn't like that look; it usually didn't bode well for me.

"Alright. How about a little tit for tat? I'll get you into the wedding. Before the fight I had with the doc, I had already RSVPed with a 'plus one.' It would be so, so rude to decline now. I can put a call into their planner and get your name substituted for the doc's. But if I do this, then you have to come with me to the doc's house to snoop a little.

I weighed my options. I knew when I was bested. She would take me to the wedding, but not without some sort of compensation. Would she and the doc make up before the wedding? Probably, but it would be good for him to realize she wasn't a pushover, that she would go ahead and make plans without him. Would it be a little awkward to change my name for the doc's? Probably a little.

Sarah had both hands in her hair. It was good and messed up at this point. I think she really was nervous over all this. "But Katie, we're good after this, and we are most *definitely* going shopping for this wedding!"

Chapter Twelve

What does "Black Tie Wedding, but not mandatory" mean? Confusing, I know. What it means is 'please wear a tux if you're a man, but if you don't have one and don't want to go out and buy one, we'd prefer you attend anyway.' For ladies, it means cocktail attire, short or long dress. White Tie for men equals a long gown for women...and if you're a member of the peerage, a tiara.

If you thought bridezillas were bad, teen girls annoying, or even mama grizzlies dangerous, they have *nothing* on Sarah Deloro when on a shopping mission

"We don't have time to go into the city," Sarah declared, meaning New York. "We'll make do with Nordstroms." We were on our way to West Farms Mall; she was driving. She was an aggressive driver, or would it be called rude? She changed lanes often, cut people off, cursed at those going too slow. Yikes. I'd been in a car with her before, and she wasn't this bad. Was something bothering her?

"Something bothering you, Sarah?" She scowled.

A quick glance at me. "You're taking this whole thing with the Di'Rissi family too lightly, Katie. They are powerful, scary, ruthless people. I can't caution you enough. But I imagine you will still go in with guns a blazing, and this time, well, once again, you're taking me with you. Only this time, it's not amusing fun and games. Please, please realize this." She snuck another look at me, almost pleading, as she cut off yet another car. I gripped the grab bar to steady myself.

"Ah, sure, Sarah," I wheezed. But she had finally gotten through to me. I knew we needed to help Addalee, but I was scared now. Not so much for myself, but I had Ellis to think of. I was being too cavalier with her safety.

"Maybe you're right, Sarah," I conceded. "I'm good and truly scared now. We don't have to go to the wedding."

She slowed down and exited the highway toward the mall. She pulled up to a red light and turned her body toward me. "Oh, we're going to the wedding, Manet. I love Addie too, and I love a good adventure—I just want to make sure you know what's at stake."

Gulp, message received. I found a beautiful dress, well, I guess I should say, 'Sarah found a beautiful dress for me.' I loved it. I don't know if I have ever had a dress as lovely, and that includes my wedding dress. It was a navy sheath, made of the thinnest of silk, with a small bit of draping at the waist to hide any imperfections, but these days I had a pretty flat stomach. It was sleeveless, but I purchased a navy woven cashmere wrap that was as light as butterfly wings. I toyed with snazzy shoes, as my dress was so elegant and simple, I ultimately went with navy sling-back pumps that were made of buttery leather. I was really and truly excited.

"What are you wearing, Sarah?" I ventured. We were on the way home. She had calmed down considerably, as I had sworn on my life that I'd behave at the wedding.

Sarah smiled. "My attire will be a surprise, but be prepared to be amazed!" Then she cackled. "The good doctor will be green with envy when he sees my Insta posts."

"Still on the outs?" I quired.

"Yes." Her face clouded, and she gave her head a little twist, making her elegant diamond earrings dance. If there was anything of Sarah's I coveted, it was her earring collection. The round stud in each ear was at least a carat, and the pear-shaped dangling pendant attached to the stud was at least two...for each earring! I know!

* * *

As much fun as we had shopping, now was the time for me to pay my dues to Sarah for my wedding plus one ticket. Before going home, we were headed to the good doctor's house.

I…can't…..believe…I'm doing this, I thought thirty minutes later. I am an educated woman. I have a thriving business. I'm a mother, a girlfriend (I still hope so), a daughter. What the heck am I doing crawling in the air ducts of a man's home where I have absolutely no business being? Not to mention, I'm committing this act of, okay, let's just say it, 'breaking and entering,' with my *high school* nemesis turned…*friend?* What the heck?

"Can you be any louder, Katie? Sheesh!" Sarah scolded as she tried and basically failed to look over her shoulder. We were actually crawling in the air conditioning duct of Dr. Dreamy's massive house.

Sarah had it in her head that the Doc was cheating on her. They had made the commitment to see only each other, and Sarah, being Sarah, was suspicious when Dr. D had gotten a call recently on his cell, thus the current fight they were engaged in. She could hear that the caller was a woman, and apparently, Dr. D had said it was a male co-worker. Why not just say it was a female co-worker? She had had so many dysfunctional relationships in her past that she was always looking for the problem. At least this was my opinion; she made issues even if there weren't any.

I sometimes felt as if I were Ethel in the Lucy and Ethel friendship, just going along with whatever craziness Sarah pulled me into. The difference? Lucy and Ethel actually *liked* each other. I told Sarah my thoughts right before we entered Dr. D's house, and she laughed with mirth. I neglected to examine the fact that in twenty-four hours, I would be the operator in another caper at the Di'Rissi wedding.

"Not too far off, Manet, except you're Lucy, and I'm Ethel. Granted, I'm slimmer, but you're the one with the crazy ideas." I cocked a brow at her. Really? She said this as we are breaking into her boyfriend's house.

How did she talk me into this crazy caper? I knew the answer. I wanted to go to the wedding; I just didn't want to admit the reason I was here. I knew I needed a sidekick, and truly, although I hated to say it, she was the best. I love Jen, but she just had too many scruples. You couldn't say that about

Sarah.

Why the air ducts? Well…that wasn't the plan, but when Dr. D came home early, and we were trapped in the laundry room with nowhere to hide. Sarah knew that it was only a matter of time before he came in here, as he liked to get out of his scrubs as soon as he got home and pop them in the washer. She knew from the final house inspection during the purchase of the doc's home (she was his realtor) that there was a crawl space to the air conditioner duct system. We could hide there until Dr. D either went back to work or moved onto an area of the house where we could escape.

Sarah had it in her head that there would be some sort of incriminating information somewhere in the house, Dr. D's computer, iPad, notes by his landline; yes, he still had a landline; he was a doctor after all.

Right before we entered with the key Dr. D had given Sarah, so it really wasn't breaking and entering, I asked Sarah, "Why don't you just ask him about the caller and what was going on with him?

Sarah smiled at me wirily as she slid the key in the lock, "Now where would the fun in that be?"

"I put my hand on her arm. "Seriously, Sarah."

She had chosen the family room door, as it faced the back of the house, and she thought the doc had a Ring doorbell camera in the front but not the back. Obviously, a mistake by the homeowner.

"If it's bad," Sarah confided, "I want time to think to compose myself." It was the most vulnerable I had ever seen Sarah.

Okay, I was good with that. I motioned 'carry on' with my hand, and we entered the house and into the spacious open concept home. Sarah went straight to the Doc's office. It was very luxurious, all dark wood, burgundy carpets, and big furniture. I sniffed for the cigar smoke that seemed like it should be present, but didn't detect any.

I hot-footed it behind her, "Sarah," I stage-whispered. "What about an alarm?" I didn't hear the tell-tale 'beep, beep' when we entered, but maybe the house had a silent alarm.

Sarah looked over her shoulder at me as she quick-stepped toward the Doc's desk situated in front of a big bay window. "He almost never sets the alarm, and he obviously didn't today." Well, alrighty then.

Sarah sat down at the cherry wood desk and reached for the doctor's computer. Hello…password? But she had that also. Who was this woman? Just as she was getting going, we heard a key in the lock. Cleaning lady, delivery? Oh my gosh, could it be the Doctor himself?

Sarah had the presence of mind to close the email page and return the computer to the home screen before she dragged me to the closest room…the laundry room. She couldn't have picked a room with an outside exit door? I thought meanly and irrationally.

We heard humming, and Sarah mouthed, "It's him!" Her eyes were huge and frankly panicked. At this point, I didn't know the Doc's habit of going straight to the laundry room to remove his scrubs, so I wasn't as frantic as Sarah. Besides, he had given her a key. Couldn't she just say she had left something here and came to fetch it, and oh, her wacky friend was along for the ride to retrieve whatever? But she had panicked, and that option was behind us. She looked around like a caged animal. Then her eyes lit on the access door to the duct system like a woman on a diet looks at chocolate cake.

"In here," she commanded as she opened the tiny metal door.

"Ah, no," I whispered as I shook my head and almost laughed. Was she serious? But then I heard footsteps approach, and they were almost upon us. The person was also whistling. Sarah heard and nodded her head. "It's for sure him!" She mouthed again. She crawled into the space, and God help me, I followed. My thought as we entered, and then I shut the mesh-type door behind us, was that it would have been so much easier to say, 'Hello' to the Doctor.

No sooner had I closed the door than I could see him through the mesh as he stripped down to his skivvies, tossed his scrubs into the washer, and started the cycle. He was one of those people who used the detergent that was on a sheet of paper. Better for the environment, no plastic bottles to recycle, just an envelope to toss in the recycle bin. And *why* am I focusing on such mundane tasks? So, I wouldn't focus on the fact that I was looking at my friend's boyfriend in his underwear. I couldn't look away until Sarah bopped me on the arm and mouthed "Stop!" She waved me on to go deeper into the crawl space.

The passage let us out by some stairs that went down to the basement. It was cold down here. I looked around, wondering if Sarah was thinking what I was, about the last time we had been in a basement together. Our eyes met, and she grinned. Yeah, she remembered. No time for that now, we had to get out of this ridiculous situation. It didn't appear that the good doctor was going out anytime soon, but then we didn't expect him home either. Sarah must have gotten the details wrong about his schedule. She was right, he was definitely acting in a suspicious manner.

I wandered around the neat basement, boxes and boxes of labeled items, old furniture stacked and covered precisely, and then…a mechanical bow and a quiver of arrows. Oh my God. Could the doc have had anything to do with Clyde's death? I looked at Sarah, and she looked at me.

"Not exactly what I thought we might find, if anything. He couldn't possibly," her eyes filled, "could he?"

"Sarah, it's silly to jump to conclusions. So, the Doc has a bow and arrow in his basement, so he's never mentioned to you that he's into archery….wait, did he ever mention it?" I was suddenly hopeful.

She shook her head no, ever so slightly. Her shoulders slumped. "This is what I get for snooping—more questions. I was thinking he was cheating on me, and I really had no proof, just my own insecurities. And if you ever remind me, I said that or tell anyone else, I said that, I'll have your hide, Katie. I mean it." I knew she did. No need to tell me twice; I shivered.

We wandered around, and I knew Sarah wanted to look in the boxes, but she refrained. I have to admit, I wanted to snoop too. Seems at odds; we came to snoop, then she ignores the boxes in the basement. That Sarah Deloro was a puzzle. We finally heard the slam of a door.

"Think we can make our escape? I whispered. She put down a book she had been flipping through onto a dusty bookshelf.

"Yeah, pretty sure that was the front door. Let's go up the house stairs, though." She said with a self-deprecating grin.

"What will you say when he asks why you were at the house? I'm sure he'll see you on the ring doorbell."

"Something tells me he won't ask." This time, there was no smile on her face.

Chapter Thirteen

This is for the wedding guests. Be a good and polite guest. Sit where you are requested to sit for either the ceremony, the reception, or both. If you are assigned a specific seat at a specific table, sit there. If you are able to choose your seat at a numbered table, do so...but never, ever, take it upon yourself to move another guest's personal items or place card to take their seat. Yes, believe it or not, I've seen it happen, more than once.

The next morning, Ellis informed me that her crew was coming over after their respective sports practices: Candy, lacrosse player extraordinaire, Kara, cheer captain, and Peter, computer geek (no practice required) and honorary little brother to all three girls. Kevin would be joining the group, and Ellis asked me to bake my famous chocolate cream cheese brownies. Did I mention that I love my daughter, but hate to bake? My contribution to the get-together was truly a labor of love.

The doorbell started ringing about seven, after the kids had been home to shower and have dinner with their families. Candy was the first to arrive, and she enveloped me in a big hug when I opened the door for her.

"Mrs. L!" she said somewhere in the vicinity of my neck; she was a whole head taller than I. I've missed you! Hard to get Ellis and Kevin to separate for more than an hour, though!" She came in, bringing a wave of cold, sweet fall air with her.

"I'm so glad you're here, now, Candy!" I smiled brightly. She was such a warm-hearted girl. She shrugged out of her letterwoman's jacket. Then, before I could properly pull Candy in and shut the front door, Kara and

Peter were on my doorstep. They both embraced me, and I took their coats.

Ellis came bouncing down the stairs and greeted her friends and then invited them into our great room. I heard giggles and guffaws, and soon Kevin had joined the mix. I went into the kitchen to make some of my popcorn, always on the stovetop, never in the microwave, and then added lots of butter and salt. I took a huge bowl of corn as well as individual bowls, along with an assortment of waters and sodas for the group. They already had their books out—wow!

"Mom! Thanks so much, but where are the brownies? You know they're Kara's favorites!"

"Coming right up!" I turned around for the brownies, plates, and napkins. But I paused when I heard the voices drop and just had to listen before I grabbed the goodies.

"Well, that's not what I heard." This from the assertive Candy. "Josie Rosetti said her uncle wasn't taking new patients because he has cancer. So, I don't think it's anything personal to your dad, Pete."

Rosetti, Rosetti…could that be Sarah's Dr. Rosetti? Cancer? Oh no! Could that be his big secret and not another woman? I would have to find a way to tell Sarah and not upset her.

Who was I kidding? That didn't seem like a possibility. Poor Sarah, poor Doc.

* * *

The next morning found Sarah Deloro and I walking along the Connecticut River. I had brought coffee in Stanley mugs for each of us. We were both bundled up against the now cold fall morning, with me in a sweatshirt and sweatpants, and a sleek Lulu Lemon matching yoga outfit and super tech jacket for Sarah.

I had invited Sarah under the guise of getting some exercise and not always meeting at Jen's. She was an active person, and actually, I needed some exercise. I wasn't happy about what I wanted to share with Sarah, who wants to hear that your significant other may have a serious illness, and the fact that he wasn't being honest with you.

"Let's sit for a minute, Sarah," I wheezed. She snorted.

"Too much for you, Manet?" She sat on a big, smooth rock. I joined her, although the rock was cold.

"Sarah..." I started, but didn't know how to finish.

Sarah stopped looking out at the Connecticut River and turned to me with a questioning eye. "Spit it out, Katie."

"I think instead of your doctor cheating on you, or being Clyde's murderer, he's sick, Sarah."

Sarah stood up. Turning to me almost angrily. "What?"

I grabbed Sarah's arm and pulled her back down onto the rock. She sat with surprisingly little resistance. "Ellis had some friends over to study last night..."

Sarah turned to me with irritation. "And this matters because?"

"They were talking about a friend named 'Josie Rosetti' and one of the kids said her uncle was sick." Here I paused. "That he has..." I gulped I didn't want to her hurt, but I would want to know. "Cancer."

Sarah was silent. She looked straight ahead. Then I felt her hand take mine.

Chapter Fourteen

If you're using real candles, with a flame, don't light them too early. You don't want them to burn down before the night is done. A good time to light the candles is during Cocktail Hour. If you don't have a planner or a formal caterer, make sure you have plenty of torches on hand, and ask a friend to light them. Pack the torches with all your decorations so you don't forget them.

Thursday found me in the role of not amateur sleuth, but that of secretary or Girl Friday to Sarah, as we navigated the best way to be supportive of Sarah's beau, Dr. Rosetti. You would think that a doctor would have all the ins and outs covered for his/her illness, but anyone can be surprisingly vulnerable. It became increasingly obvious to me that everyone, it matters not who you are, needs an advocate in this delicate situation. I thought Sarah might skip out on me for the wedding tomorrow, but she was ready to go the next night with no fuss at all. I think it was her way of saying, "thank you." I never really thought about it, but she didn't seem to have anyone. I knew that her dad had died in a car accident when she was in high school, and her mom moved down to Florida when I was in California. I didn't quiz her; I was just there, her friend.

* * *

I have only done one reception at this wedding venue. But let's just say it's a different world when one is a guest here versus being a vendor. The venue?

The Cork Spring Country Club in Rosewood, MA. We didn't, in fact, go to the Di'Rissi Wedding ceremony. It was a Catholic Mass, and while I'm Catholic, Sarah is not, and she wasn't feeling it.

It only took us an hour's drive, but I was thinking we should maybe Uber home. I wanted to Uber here, but Sarah wouldn't have it. I think it was a control thing. I'm not sure how she drove in her dress. Bluntly, it looked as if she had been sewn into it. I was going to get a good look at her dress as soon as we handed her car over to the valet, and she was standing upright. She was planning our poses for her photos to send the doc on the way over, but her motivation was different than two days ago. Two days ago, she had wanted to make him jealous. Now, she just wanted to make him smile. Dr. Rosetti had thyroid cancer, which was very curable and had a high survival rate. He was deep into his radiation therapy and was fatigued. But the prognosis was great. It had brought Sarah and him closer. He was learning, as I had, what a good support and friend she could be.

The valet zoomed off with Sarah's car, and I got the full effect of her dress. It was black, low-cut, and very short. She had the figure for it. It clung to every curve, and would have highlighted any imperfection, but then…there were none.

"Sarah, you don't disappoint. Dr. Dreamy is going to do his best to never make you mad."

I don't know what I expected as a reply, but she was surprisingly humble, and well, pleased. "Thanks, Katie," was all I got.

The doors were opened immediately by two smiling club employees, "Welcome," they enthused. We smiled our thanks. The Cocktail Hour Music assaulted our scenes, well, at least mine. It was just a little too loud, and definitely too loud to have any kind of conversation.

The music was very festive and nostalgic. If I wasn't mistaken, that was ol' Blue Eyes crooning over the loudspeakers. I imagine we'd have live music soon. We were a little early, having not come from the church.

A server approached us with a tray of champagne. We both snagged a glass and smiled our thanks. I looked over our server's shoulder, and yes, yes, there was one of those tacky girls with a unit on her skirt where she had glasses of champagne stacked on and around her. It was more or less a mental cage with fabric over the cage and then shelf spacing where full glasses of champagne were stored. I'm not sure how she walked without spilling, but she appeared to have a nice cadence down. Ever seen one? I've only seen one other in the wild, but I've heard about them. To each his own.

Next up were white gloved servers with trays of hors d'oeuvres. We both declined, and I swear the servers seemed disappointed. Another guest wedding tip: *Do NOT place your used toothpicks, napkins, or glasses on a server's tray of fresh appetizers.* Yes, this does happen.

Sarah and I found the round table with our table assignments and place cards. The cards were arranged precisely and beautifully. There was a giant floral arrangement in the center of the table, and it was stunning. The flowers were fresh and plump. I wouldn't be surprised if they were sourced from a local flower farm. They were all seasonal flowers too, in differing shades of cream and white. There were many dahlias, asters, and roses. I must get the name of their florist; they were a wonder.

We entered the grand ballroom. I estimated the guest list topped three hundred, as there had to be at least thirty tables of ten in here. It took a minute, but we found our table, thirteen. No, I'm not superstitious, but I still got the shivers from our table number.

"Yay!" I beamed at Sarah. We get to pick our own seats at the table. We would want to reserve our choices now, before the other guests got there. We should be facing the sweetheart table, so we don't have to spend the night craning our necks to listen to speeches or watch parent dances. The 'sweetheart table,' directly in front of the dance floor, is where all the action would take place.

Sarah nodded at me in agreement. She was not going to challenge my wedding knowledge—well, it was common sense, really. We both placed our name cards in front of our dinner plates.

"Okay, mission accomplished. Let's go join the party."

"I know you are the wedding expert here, Katie, but you're my guest. Don't steal my thunder!" I wasn't sure if she was kidding, serious, or mad. That Sarah Deloro was hard to read.

She punched me in the arm. "Kidding, Manet, but it wouldn't hurt to put your wedding hat away for tonight. You may think no one is listening, but someone, somewhere in all this mess is listening. It's their job. And I don't want it said my plus one was a criticizing know-it-all wedding planner.

Sarah was right. I was uber critical, and I had to watch myself. I was worried about gaucheness. How about the guest who is vocal in her contempt of what she thinks is an overdone wedding? I have to remember what I always tell my brides, there is no right or wrong with weddings, just what you and your fiancé like, as long as you don't hurt anyone's feelings. But those elevated centerpieces were sure hurting my feelings. Okay, last one. I'd stop now; shame on me.

We entered the fray, and the Cocktail Hour music was warming up. You'd never know these people had just come from church. They were drinking like fish. Our friend, the champagne lady, was running on empty. Someone needed to refill her skirt, stat!

It was time to get the Di'Rissi family tree down from Sarah. "So, where did Clyde fit into all this. Was his girl, Maria, a sister of the bride, a cousin, what?"

Sarah stopped her procession into the main party area, grabbed my arm, stopping mine.

"Okay, quick tutorial. Anthony, 'Ant,' Di'Rissi is the father of the bride, the mob boss. He's the son of the family business founder, Joseph Di'Rissi," she hissed. Ant's married to Sophia, a sweet little Italian lady born in Italy. They have six children, but the only ones you need to be aware of are: Maria, ex of Clyde, Ruby, today's bride, Diamond, the maid of honor, and Anthony Jr., 'Tony.' The other three are in high school and one college senior, so they won't make a bleep on your radar, unless you want to do their weddings in a few years." She resumed walking, smiling at guests, waving to others. She was a celebrity.

"Let's get some air," she said over her shoulder to me. She was right. As more and more people made their way into the Cocktail Hour space, it was getting quite warm. I felt overstimulated with all the voices, colors, fragrances, food smells, and music. We made our way out a set of French doors and onto a stone balcony overlooking one of the golf course greens. The night was perfect, just warm enough outside that they didn't need the tall heaters they had at the ready, but not too hot by any means. I wish the event manager would try to get more people out here. We leaned over the balcony and both of us gazed upward. We couldn't see many stars, too many trees, too much lighting in the area, but the sky was clear. If I were with anyone else, it would be…romantic, ha!

That's when it happened. Two men came bursting through another set of French doors; the long room housed six sets of such doors. It was dark on the balcony, with only small votive candles illuminating the scattered café-sized tables placed around the spacious balcony.

One tuxedoed man seemed to be holding the other by his black bow tie. The 'holder' was the larger of the two men, and if I'm not mistaken, slightly balding.

"You son of a bitch! How could you have let this happen? You *knew* how much Maria loved him! It's your job to keep this type of thing from happening! Are you telling me that that's what happened? Are you sure? Are you sure without a shadow of a doubt?"

Sarah and I instinctively moved closer together. What does one do in a situation such as this? Do we try to sneak out? Do we stay and quietly listen? Yikes.

"Do we stay, or do we go?" I resisted the urge to start singing the old song by the very name and the urge to giggle. I too often giggled when I was nervous.

So, we did nothing. The men continued to argue. "How was I supposed to know that he would *kill* him?" Little Man wheezed out.

Baldy shook Little Man by the collar. "Because it's your *job* to know, that's why." He threw Little Man down on the terrace floor and stalked off. Little Man stood with the aid of one of the patio chairs, dusted himself off, straightened his tux jacket and bow tie, and reentered the Cocktail space.

Sarah moved away from me and gave me a look as if to say, 'what the heck are you doing standing so close to me?' Then she frowned.

"The bigger bald guy…was Anthony Di'Rissi." She gestured toward the open French doors like Vanna White on 'Wheel of Fortune.' "Shall we?"

I grabbed her arm. "Wait!" I heard the desperation in my own voice. "I have so many questions! What was that all about?"

"I have my suspicions, but I don't care, Katie. I warned you about this. I knew this wedding was a fishing trip for you, but there are certain things that are off limits, and what you just witnessed is one of them. Now let's go inside and get a good spot to see the grand entrance. I'll even let you lead the way and pick the spot because I don't want to hear you whine that you 'know more than I do about weddings,' yada yada," I stepped around her and reentered the room first, but not before I shot her a look of loathing.

I picked a spot directly across from where the wedding party would enter. No sooner had we taken our spots, having been briefly jostled by a drunken tuxedo clad frat boy, than the band leader announced the first members of the wedding party—the parents of the groom. They were very cute, short, round, and smiley. The bridesmaids and groomsmen entered in pairs, the men, clad in traditional black tuxedos, the women in Pepto Bismol pink. My favorite, ah, no. But as I have to do with the weddings I plan, I remind myself, 'it's not your wedding, Katie.' I was impressed that the bride had so many friends to include. She had fifteen bridesmaids and six children in her bridal party. WOW!

I looked at Sarah and made big eyes. She glared and then laughed. "Fourteen of those girls are her sisters and cousins. I know, crazy, right? This is a big ole Italian wedding with a twist of Mob.

The band was terrific; I appreciated it as we moved into the dining space after the boring speeches. Anthony Di'Rissi cried as he toasted his daughter and new son-in-law. I wonder if he cried when he, (if stories were to be believed), executed his enemies. Doubtful.

We were seated with other business owners from our community; there was Benny Winston from the Pawn Shop in Hartford and his sweet wife, Bunny. Next to them were the Lamaches, owners of the Sip and Save package store in East Hartford, as well as four cousins I had a feeling the wedding planner didn't know where to place.

The wine flowed, and tongues loosened. We learned that two of the four cousins at our table would never forgive the bride for excluding them from the wedding party. And that the main reason they were excluded was that their dad wasn't producing as much as required. No one seemed to want or need an explanation. I, however, was very curious. I opened my mouth once, when they were discussing the situation, and felt a sharp kick in my shin from none other than the sharp-pointed toes of Sarah Deloro. She squeezed my wrist as she kicked me, a warning not to yell out in pain. I'd get my revenge.

Dinner was followed by the cake cutting with much music and cheering. The groom succumbed to peer pressure and smashed the cake into the bride's face. It was one of the most aggressive cake cuttings I've ever seen. In fact, it's rare that either party smashes the cake anymore. Today, there isn't always a wedding cake at the reception. Sometimes, couples opt for a less traditional dessert. Guests seem to like the alternative desserts, but I, with my sentimental heart, love a wedding cake. In fact, when Ellis gets married, we are going to buy a cake that will serve double our guest head count and use the cake as not just a dessert, but also a decorative item. Cheaper than excess flowers!

Was smashing of the wedding cake, all the way up to the bride's nose, an Italian tradition, or a Mob one? Or was it just that the groom was a jerk? The guests seemed to love it, though, and the bride laughed, so who was I to criticize?

I saw Little Man get up and leave his table, headed to the men's room? I saw my opportunity and rose from our table.

"Ladies' Room," I said to Sarah. "Wanna go?"

"What are we, thirteen?" She snipped.

I knew if I asked her to go with me, she wouldn't. Had I stood up and tried to make my getaway, she'd be all over me, at least give me a lecture. Ha! Outsmarted!

I smiled my way out of the ongoing conversation, now focused on the bride and groom's Honeymoon in Hawaii, and headed out of the ballroom toward where I thought the ladies' room would be. But I was really interested in…the men's room, as I wanted to somehow grill Little Man.

I went the wrong way at first, of course I did, but I eventually found the restrooms. They were a bit out of the way, which surprised me. I rounded the last corner and saw my prey exiting the men's room. I smiled at him as we passed, and then, oops! Twisted my ankle on those darn high-heeled pumps. I was taking a risk. What if he wasn't paying attention? I was in danger of going down, and with this thick pile of carpet, I'm not sure I could pivot and save myself. But Lady Luck was with me. He caught me, quite expertly, I may add. He released me, very respectfully. Some men in that situation will hold on a little too long.

I could feel my face flush; even though the situation was manufactured, I was embarrassed.

"I am so sorry and thank you!" I met his eyes and smiled. He smiled back. I still got it. "Those shoes will get you every time, especially on these carpets." He grinned then, and he had a gold tooth, I kid you not. It was kind of…fascinating.

"I'm so glad you were here," I all but batted my eyelashes at him.

"Buy you a drink," he came back with, kinda funny as it was an open bar.

"Sure!" I said with enthusiasm.

We grabbed our drinks from the overworked bartender in the cocktail space. We found a high-top table away from the bar line, as well as the band. I love bands, but they are almost always too loud. As a planner, I am constantly asking them to lower the volume. They rarely do.

So, what did I want to find out from the man trying so hard to charm me right now? Well, why was the father of the bride tussling with him at his own daughter's wedding? And who killed whom? When 'Ant' said Maria had loved him, my mind went right to Boyd.

I smiled, my Katie smile. It seemed to work; he smiled back, although I'm not sure I was happy with the type of smile he returned. I didn't want to give him the wrong idea…but, I did want info. I looked over my shoulder and caught Sarah's eye. She shook her head at me but smiled slightly.

"Friend of the bride's family?" I asked with what I hoped was an innocent air.

He winked at me, yes, he did. "Yeah, and a business associate."

I looked down at my glass of wine and batted my eyes. I kinda hated myself. "I thought I saw you before, goofing around with the father of the bride."

He chuckled, but his face turned red. "Yeah, well, boys will be boys, ya know."

"I think it's kind of exciting." I blushed and looked down again, but not for the reason he probably thought. I was just a wee bit disgusted with myself. This is for Addalee, I reminded myself.

I could almost see his chest puff. "I don't think we have been properly introduced. I'm Gene."

"Kate," I responded, smiling. "So, what was the big hullabaloo with the father of the bride?"

"Ah, just high emotions, ya know, his kid getting married and all. We play rough."

I put my hand on his arm. "Want to do a shot?" I knew that most establishments didn't allow shots at occasions such as these, but it was worth a try to loosen him up.

"Hell, yeah," He grinned. He sauntered over to the bar, passed something to the bartender, and came back to me with four shot glasses. We 'cheered' and when he tipped his head back, I poured mine on the floor and then tipped my head to match his. This clumsy motion wouldn't have worked on a more sober partner, but 'Gene' was already three sheets to the wind.

He grinned at me; I grinned back. Sarah, who had moved to a position where I could see her without turning, shook her head at me. This time, she wasn't smiling. So, what?

Gene picked up his second shot. I mirrored him. We clicked glasses again, and I repeated my move. No one noticed, but I'd have to alert the staff to the 'spill' so no one slipped. Always the planner, am I.

Gene went to get refills, and I grabbed a passing server and begged a towel. She luckily had one tossed over her shoulder, and I stealthily dropped in on the floor to absorb my spills. Gene came back with four more shots. Jeeze, that guy. Sarah was getting ready to come over, but I gave her a tiny 'no' shake of my head. She held up two fingers, meaning, I think, she was giving me two minutes before she swooped in to 'save the day.' I wasn't a child,

Sarah! I thought.

Gene downed two shots in a row, and didn't seem to notice, or care that I wasn't joining in. He smiled sloppily at me. This was too easy.

"Gene," I placed my hand again on his forearm. "What's the deal with that dead photographer?"

He shook his head, "Yeah, that was unfortunate. Wrong place, wrong time. Never a good idea to eavesdrop. Especially with this crew." And he face-planted on the bistro table. I saw it coming, so I had just enough time to remove the pretty little centerpiece, so he didn't crack his head on it. Sarah *did* come over then.

"Okay, Cinderella, time to catch the pumpkin coach home." What? That makes no sense.

"Okay, that wasn't a good one, but it's time to go, Chica." I knew she was right. We went back to our assigned table, grabbed our wraps and pocketbooks, and high-tailed it out of there. We didn't even thank the bride's family, a glaring faux pas in my book, but probably for the best.

Chapter Fifteen

Speeches. In all honesty, the wedding speeches are the guests' least favorite part of the wedding. Make sure all your toast-givers and speechmakers know their time limit and practice for it. And under no circumstances, let an 'Open Mic' situation take place! A new trend is to have the speeches, except for the 'Parent Welcome Toast,' the night before at the Rehearsal Dinner.

Today was an awkward meeting with Charlie and Remley. They were seated in front of my desk in the visitors' chair. Remley was weepy and wiping her eyes and nose with a tissue that had seen better days. I picked up the tissue box I always had on my desk and offered it to her. She wrinkled her nose and shook her head 'no.'

Fine, use your dirty little scrap of tissue.

"What are we going to do, Charlie?" She grabbed his arm. I could see the irritation on his face, but also saw how hard he tried to tamp it down.

Charlie took a deep breath; he turned to her with deliberation. "Remley. It's sad, very sad, that Clyde was murdered. But we've talked about this. There are a hundred other photographers out there that can take our wedding photos."

"He's right, Remley, I have a great list of photographers. We will find someone who meets your needs."

"Shut up, Kate, no one asked you," Remley said with venom in her voice.

WOW. I stood up. "I think we'd better continue this meeting at a later time when you're feeling more like yourself, Remley, because your behavior is not acceptable. I'll show you to the door."

"Are you kidding me? You work for us, Kate. We tell *you* when the meeting's up."

"I'm so sorry, Katie." Charlie stood up and placed a hand on Remley's bicep to gently guide her up. "Remley's taking Clyde's death hard. Forgive her."

Remley seemed to suddenly realize her ugliness. "Sorry, Kate. On top of losing our photographer, we're closing on the new house today," more like an estate, according to Sarah. "And the bank is giving us grief on the cash sale."

Huh? Too much information, and Charlie looked stricken. He immediately looked at Remley with shock and embarrassment. What the heck? I'd have to ask Sarah about this…but, I knew she was a stickler about real estate ethics. I'd have to get it out of her another way. She was so hot and cold about her ethics regarding her clients. Depended on her mood.

"Kate's busy, Rem, let's go, and we can reschedule." I saw Remley's face turn purple with pent up rage. She wasn't a happy girl.

I escorted them out of my office and toward the reception room door.

"We'll be in touch, Katie. And I really am sorry," he said in a low voice, probably hoping Remley was too distracted to hear. I smiled weakly, but wasn't going to say it was 'okay' because it wasn't.

They left, and I fired off a text to Sarah.

So, Charlie and Remley are closing on their property today?

Typing bubbles.

Yeah

Trouble with the closing, funds???

You know I can't speak to that, Katie.

Yep. Charlie paid my retainer in cash (true). *Is that odd?* (Charlie had insisted on paying me even though I had offered to plan his wedding pro bono).

Bubbles, then nothing. Bubbles again, then nothing.

Once again, Katie, you know I can't speak to client's financials, but often using cash is a red flag, but sometimes it happens.

Bingo. She answered my question without answering my question outright.

This was weird. Granted, I hadn't purchased many properties in my day, but an entire cash purchase for the amount of Charlie's estate was crazy! Where did he get that much liquid cash? Something wasn't quite right. I have no idea what that may be, but something was off. Something was off with Remley, too.

Just then, a text came in from Charlie.

Katie, I am so so sorry for Remley's outrageous behavior. Inexcusable. She has been under lots of stress lately.

Boo-hoo, I thought.

I'll send the remainder of your fee. Ok if I drop cash by your office soon

Cash again? I thought. What was going on with Charlie?

And just like that, he answered my question.

My grandmother died recently and left me a gift. It just arrived into my account yesterday, so I am paying my bills this way.

So sorry for your loss, Charlie. I responded. Odd that he felt he needed to explain his finances to me. But maybe it was necessary due to Remley's blurting out information on the closing of their new home. It was all odd, but it made more sense to me now that he explained about the gift from his grandmother. None of my business. I rattled off my info. I'd be glad of the early payment from Charlie. It wasn't due until fifteen days before his wedding.

Chapter Sixteen

Don't forget a card box at your wedding. Some couples are opting for an online registry, either from a store or a "Honey fund." But there is a generation out there that will want to bring a card with a monetary gift to your wedding. Make sure they feel included and comfortable in their gift giving.

After my disastrous meeting with Charlie and Remley, I decided to do a little investigating. The whole thing with Charlie's financials was weird. So, I headed over to my happy place, Eastbury Jewelers. I'll lay it out there, I love jewelry. If I had unlimited wealth, a good chunk of it would go there. All of my happy sensors went off as I entered the store, and the bell on the door jingled merrily. Mr. Parker, owner of Eastbury Jewelers, was behind the glass-topped display cases as the usual, and he grinned when he saw me walk through the door.

"Hello, Miss Manet!" For as long as I've been home, I've been asking Mr. Parker to call me Katie or Mrs. Ludlow. He refused, but I guess it's fair, as he has asked me to call him by his first name, and I just can't do it. He will always be 'Mr. Parker' to me.

"Oh, Mr. Parker, it's a beaut of a day out there!" I walked to the display case nearest me and all but drooled over the emeralds. They have always been a favorite gemstone.

"I do think I'll close the shop for a half hour and take my lunch at the fountain." Our touchstone for all the locals. Brian and I had our own history with the fountain and the park-like setting around it.

"Sounds wonderful, Mr. Parker."

"What can I do ya for, Katie?" I wish I had a wedding planner errand to disguise my snooping, but I'd just have to rely on my love of jewelry to try to pry some info from Mr. Parker.

"Just looking, Mr. Parker, and I haven't seen you in a few days." He smiled at me. I knew I was a favorite.

"Are you looking for anything in particular? Maybe something in the ring department?" He made his busy grey eyebrows go up and down.

I laughed. "No, Mr. Parker," I just had a few extra minutes and wanted to say hi."

"Well, I'll leave you to your ganderings, Katie. I have some repairs in the back. Holler if you need anything."

"Will do, Mr. Parker."

I returned my lust to the emerald case, and Mr. Parker turned to go to the back room. He turned back and said, "Oh, Katie. Are you doing Charlie and Remley's wedding?"

I looked up at him. "Sure am."

"Is all good with the two of them?"

I guess Mr. Parker felt it was okay to discuss a customer vendor to vendor, because he usually wouldn't say a word about his clients. He told me at one point that he was like a priest, ha ha, and whatever was discussed in his store was in the vault.

I raised a questioning eye to him and felt my forehead crease. "As far as I know, is there something afoot, something I should know about?"

He hesitated. "Slippery slope here, Katie. But I was a little concerned when Charlie insisted on paying cash. I was okay with it, but Charlie seemed to be sort of secretive about it. Often, clients want to pay cash, so they write a check or transfer funds. But he brought it in..." he stopped. "Well, just checking in. You probably have a better handle on things than I do..." his face reddened. He had already said too much, I know he was thinking.

Oh, Charlie, what is going on? But I couldn't help but think that all this started about the same time as his relationship with Remley...

"What do you know about the blushing bride?" I asked Mr. Parker. Should

I feel guilty for gossiping about one of my couples? Probably. Not very professional, but there *were* extenuating circumstances, right? Mr. Parker wiped his hands on the green work apron that he wore when the shop was slow, or he was working in the back.

"Well, I do know she's not a local girl. In fact, I don't think she's even from New England. Pretty sure she's from….I want to say, maybe Kentucky. Conservative views. Excited to be married and be a mom."

"Wow, Mr. Parker, you gather a lot of intel when folks are in your shop." I chucked.

"Her mother is coming up in a couple weeks and is going to stay until the wedding…with Charlie and Remley."

I did a 'no-no' and leaned my forearms on the glass display case toward Mr. Parker.

"You're just showing off now, Mr. Parker." I smiled at him.

He laughed gently. "What can I say, I like to chat *and* listen."

"Tell me more," I goaded him.

"I got the impression that she was used to a lot, either that or she was just naturally…" he stopped. Either professionalism or kindness made him stop.

But not me. I wasn't going to hold back. She was awful to me last time we met, and I wasn't feeling particularly forgiving. I just may step back from doing their wedding. I haven't decided yet. An apology was definitely required.

"Wanted a big ol' ring, huh, Mr. Parker?" I needled. I could see the wheels in his head turning. As their planner, I had surely seen the ring. It would break no confidentiality if we chatted about 'the ring,' I imagined him thinking.

He took a breath, then said, "The stones I had in house weren't good enough for Miss Remley, and I have some beauts. Had to order a stone from my wholesaler. You've seen the ring, right, Katie?" he was starting to feel guilty; I couldn't let him.

"Oh, for sure! It's gorgeous! What is it?" I pretended to nonchalantly examine the ruby case. " Four, five carats, in platinum?"

"You have a good eye, Katie. The main stone is five carats, and the side baguettes are another two carats, one on each side. Then the wedding band…oh my gosh. It's an eternity band made of four more carats of round diamonds. And yes, all set in platinum.

"No wonder you thought it odd Charlie paid for all that in cash," I mused. I wouldn't go as far as to ask the price. Why make both of us uncomfortable when he refused to divulge that information? We both liked Charlie, but something didn't ring true.

"Same deal last week. It was Remley's birthday and Charlie picked out a truly unique piece—a diamond bracelet—ten carats in total. And again, cash."

Didn't Charlie just text me that his grandmother's legacy 'just arrived in his account *yesterday*'? Oh, Charlie, what have you gotten yourself into?

Chapter Seventeen

If you choose to have a First Dance, or a Parent Dance (Father/Daughter, Mother/Son), remember, you do not have to dance to the entire length of the song unless you want to. Your entertainment can truncate it for you if you wish.

I bade farewell to Mr. Parker and walked home. Remley was very much on my mind. What was her story? I wasn't even positive when and where Charlie had met her. All I knew was that the town (and I!) was surprised when he announced his engagement. We had seen no first dates, heard no rumors—unusual in our small little burg. Sure, they both went to Georgetown, but that was a long time ago.

I walked into my mudroom and took my Bean Boots off. I wore my LL Bean boots about ten months of the year. I padded through the kitchen and turned on the espresso machine, an upgrade for sure from my Keurig. I flipped on the hot pot for hot water so I could make an Americano with the espresso I would soon brew. But first, I washed my hands and disinfected my phone. I've been doing this since the Covid lockdown, and I had been pretty healthy. I brewed my two shots of espresso, added hot water, and carried my cup to my home office. I fired up my computer once I settled into my desk chair. I was going to do a deep dive on Remley. And what better way to do so than a good look at her social media?

Facebook or Instagram, which to look at first? I went to Facebook. I typed her name into the search bar, and she came right up. We weren't friends, and she had her account set to private, as any sane person would. I couldn't see much but the frequent changes to her profile pic. Okay, then, onto Instagram. I wasn't sure how lucky I'd be, as it would be kinda weird to ask for a friend request now, as we hadn't ended our last conversation on the best of terms. I had never checked, but with Charlie being an attorney, I doubted he had much of a social media presence. I was soon to find out.

I searched Remley on Insta…and guess what? She was public! I wasn't sure why, but unbeknownst to me, she had a little business she was hawking, or had been hawking before her engagement, it appeared. Remley…was a professional organizer! Was that how Charlie met her? Had she come into his home and 'organized him'? I scrolled all the way to the beginning of her account. She had had the account for a while. If I had to guess, I'd say she was in her late thirties. Mr. Parker was right; she was from Kentucky and did go to Georgetown University. I scrolled through all the food and travel posts until I got to the 'organizing' stuff. And then I found the beginning of Charlie and Remley. Usually, I ask for info about how my couples met, etc., but it felt weird to do so as I knew Charlie so well. If he had volunteered…but he hadn't.

So long story short, while they had gone to the same university, they met at an all-inclusive singles resort in the Caribbean. Who knew? That didn't seem like a 'Charlie thing,' but apparently it was. I can imagine he was lonely, and it's hard to meet people in our small town. I had mixed feelings…was I just a little bit jealous? I knew that he had always carried a torch for me; did it bother me a little that he no longer did? I pushed that back. I didn't want to examine those thoughts.

I followed the timeline of Charlie and Remley's romance. Nothing stood out, nothing exceptional. I was disappointed. I'm not sure exactly what I hoped to find, but I found nothing unusual. Maybe I had gone through the early years too quickly. I scrolled down to past times and gave those photos a little more care. Nothing stood out in her early years, but something did more recently. In the last four years, she had posted photos with four different men, all she claimed that 'this one was *the* one.' Now *that* was odd. What I couldn't understand was why she wouldn't delete those photos. Surely Charlie would see this as odd if he looked, but maybe he hadn't…probably he hadn't. If he didn't have an Instagram account, how could he? But wouldn't one of his friends say something, razzing him about the photos? The answer was probably not. I don't know for a fact, but I don't think all that many men our age spent time going over their buddy's fiancée's Instagram. I didn't, and I had a vested interest. Weird for sure.

Chapter Eighteen

Vendor meals: if your vendor will be present during the dinner hour, they require a meal. Most put it in their contract that they be "..provided a hot meal or thirty minutes of 'off time' to go off-site for a meal if necessary." But better for all to provide a vendor meal served by your caterer. Your caterer will charge you less for vendor meals than for your guests.

Kate! *Can we meet? Brian was here again, and I'm worried— REALLY worried*

This from Addalee.

Of course! Jen's in ten? I shot back a text.

She sent a thumbs-up emoji. Okay, Addalee and I were going to have a discussion on texting…according to Ellis, a thumbs-up emoji means you are mad at the person you're texting.

I closed my laptop and reversed the steps I had just made. Back through the kitchen, into the mudroom, boots on, out the door. I beat Addalee to Jen's, so I grabbed a table. Then I went to the coffee bar and ordered two black coffees for us, no time to be fancy. We needed caffeine! Oh…and I ordered some chocolate chip cookies. Don't judge.

By the time I made it back to our table with the bounty, Addalee walked in the door, her beautiful hair windblown, her cheeks ruddy. I think today I noticed a little baby bump. She looked harried, worried, but she glowed with health and vitality. When she reached me, Addalee leaned down and hugged me, placing a kiss, which was uncharacteristic of her, on my cheek. I hugged her back. She clung to me.

"Sit, sit." I urged her. "Oh Jeeze!" I exclaimed I got you coffee. "Shall I swap it out for herbal tea?"

I had no idea what the protocol was for pregnancy these days. If Brian and I…well, all I can say *is if* I had to give up coffee for nine months again like I did when I was pregnant with Ellis, it may be a deal breaker. Just kidding…but was I? If I was selfish enough to begrudge the absence of coffee in my life, was I really ready to make all the sacrifices that being the parent of a baby and that a young child demanded? I wasn't sure I wanted to answer that question. But answer it I must, and soon. I wasn't getting any younger, and Brian for sure wasn't getting any more patient. "A cup or two is okay," she reached for the cup, but not a cookie. That's okay, more for me.

I decided to jump right in. "So, Brian's sniffing around again, huh?"

Addalee's windblown ruddy face blanched. She had her hands wrapped around her ceramic cup, and I saw the knuckles of her hands turn white as she gripped it too hard.

"I don't know why he's focusing on me so much. Yes, I'm good with a bow. Yes, Clyde and I had words, but why me?"

Was she fishing? Did she think Brian had confided in me? Was she trying to get information? That wasn't Addalee, but desperate times…

"Are you speaking metaphorically, Addie, or are you asking if I know something?"

Addalee looked stricken. "Katie! Oh, no! I am here to get comfort and advice from one of my dearest friends, not the girlfriend of the police detective."

I smiled. I knew she spoke the truth. "I'm sure the fact that you don't have an alibi is a matter of concern, Addie."

Her eyes skittered away and looked over my shoulder toward the baristas.

"Well, of course, Cory would give me one, but I don't think it would carry too much weight. Of course, he'd lie for his pregnant wife. I'd probably be on someone's ring camera anyway. I'm just so embarrassed, Katie. Cory and I shouldn't be fighting now, but we are. I always knew he was a mama's boy, but the whole 'having his mom in the delivery room' thing is taking its toll. Am I wrong to expect him to have my back?" Her eyes pleaded with me to support her. No problem there. I was beyond annoyed with Cory. What the heck. His mother had no business in the delivery room, unless it was a great wish of Addalee's. Addalee's hand went instinctively to her slightly rounded belly, and her beautiful sea-green eyes filled. The tears rolled freely down her dewy cheek unchecked. I covered her hand with my own.

"I'm sure it's not as bad as you fear, Addie, either with the police or Cory." Her face flushed again. "Well, my mother-in-law isn't helping matters. She's doing everything she can to drive a wedge between Cory and me. When I resisted her demand to be present for the baby's birth, she stopped trying to mask her disdain."

I could believe it. Cory's mom had never liked Addalee, thought she wasn't good enough for her precious son. Cory had always stood up to his family and put Addalee first. It made me wonder what had changed.

"He's always had your back, Addie. What has changed?

"It's not common knowledge, but my mother-in-law has MS, and she's really being a bear about it. She has her ups and downs, but she's putting the guilt trip on Cory and making him choose between us, not just about the delivery. She wants to come to all our doctor appointments. And if I'm being honest, I'm not always understanding. I know I should let some things go, but I'm just so emotional these days. I don't even feel I can go to Cory with my concerns over the whole murder thing." I really didn't know what to say. I'd help her, though. I had to. And a thought came.

Addalee had said it. We would look at her neighbor's Ring doorbell footage to get her an alibi. We could pinpoint her location that way and prove she wasn't anywhere near Clyde to kill him. Or so I hoped.

Chapter Nineteen

Mothers of the Groom: Remember this is not your day. The bride is not your daughter. The bride is your son's future wife. Do not wear white, off-white, cream, ecru, light silver, taupe, or light grey to the wedding. Do not make your son choose between you and his future wife. If you're lucky enough to have a daughter, you can be the mother of the bride then.

It was a warmer-than-usual Sunday in October, and I had on just a barn jacket and jeans as I walked from home to Jen's for my meeting with Charlie. It was uncomfortable, but I had to meet with him, and preferably without Remley. I had to be assured going forward that there would not be any more incidents like the one in my office when Remley had told me to 'shut up.' If Charlie couldn't guarantee that, I would have to step down as their planner. Charlie had apologized off the cuff via text, but that wasn't good enough. I had thought I needed an in-person apology from Remley, but I could forego that, as long as Charlie and I addressed it face to face. This is why one shouldn't work with friends. If this were anyone else, our business relationship would be over. No one deserves verbal abuse.

I was waiting for Charlie at my favorite table at Jen's when he walked in with a bouquet of at least two dozen yellow roses (yellow is for friendship), a giant box (and I'm talking giant) of Godiva chocolates. I knew for a fact this could be purchased at our local Barnes and Noble, but brownie points for the effort, Charlie.

He had on his attorney face; his smile was staged: humble, apologetic. Well, he should be.

But he was an old friend and had been good to me. I'd meet him halfway. I stood and graciously accepted his guilt gifts.

"Well, isn't this lovely. Thank you, Charlie," I said, giving him my cheek for his air kiss.

I rested the giant bouquet on the table, glad it was a four-top, and placed the candy on the chair next to me. "Can I get you a cup of coffee. I wasn't going to do so, but I was feeling kinder. That box of chocolates really was a nice consolation prize. He even got a smile from me.

"Gosh, no thank you, Katie. I'm all caffeinated out. But I wanted to say again, I'm so sorry for Remley's behavior. She really was distraught over the whole Clyde situation. I know it's not hard to replace a photographer, and she does, too; it's just that the whole wedding thing has her so emotional. She wants everything to be perfect. I can assure you her outburst won't be repeated."

That's all I wanted, but I think we were both being unrealistic in expecting or making that guarantee. No one could promise the behavior of another. I'd just have to get over it, for Charlie's sake. He deserved my loyalty.

"No wedding is ever perfect, Charlie. You and Remley need to know that going forward. But I will do my utmost best to make sure it's as close to perfect as possible." And here I smiled, a genuine smile.

"I put a hand on Charlie's forearm. "I didn't ask, how are you doing with all this? You had to have developed some sort of rapport with Clyde. I'm sorry you lost a friend, Charlie."

Charlie let out a puff of air. "It's hard, Katie, would be hard no matter what. But the way he died just makes it so much worse."

"For sure," I agreed. "What are your thoughts about the whole thing? Do you have any suspects in mind?"

"He leaned back in his café chair. Charlie looked tired. "I'm leaving that to the police."

"Did the police interview you?" I wasn't letting him off the hook. I had him here, was going to get any info if I could.

"I think they interviewed all his clients, so yes, they did." I had not been interviewed and thought I might be someone who had worked with him.

But then maybe Brian had had a hand in that, pretty sure I was with him that night anyway.

Would Charlie let it go, or would he deflect and name someone he thought might have done it? He was very protective of Remley. Wait, could it be her? Doubtful, but still…

"Well, you know he was dating Maria Di'Rissi, and they had a very volatile relationship." I knew that, but how did Charlie?

"Do you know her?" If Charlie thought I was being too quizzical, he didn't show it. But then he was on his best behavior.

He looked like he wanted something to do with his hands, and I bet he regretted not ordering something. Sipping a drink was perfect for taking a natural break or slowing down a conversation.

"I do. I've done a little business for her father," oh my gosh. This surprised me in a big way. I didn't see Charlie working for a mob guy. "And I've met her upon occasion. That is actually how I met Clyde. He was always at the estate when I came with papers and whatnot for Mr. Di'Rissi to sign."

"What is she like?"

Charlie pressed his lips together. Was that an unconscious tell that he felt he should 'keep his mouth closed?

"Well, not to be unkind, but she looks like her dad." Well, that said a lot. Mr. Di'Rissi was not a handsome man, but not an ogre, either. But if he were a woman, not great looking. But I already knew this as I had seen her at the wedding. "And she's angry all the time, and I mean…angry."

Yikes. "So…what was the attraction?" I thought but did not say, financial.

Charlie looked away. "Who knows about love, Katie?" And his eyes again met mine. He wasn't going to speak ill of Miss Di'Rissi, that's for sure. He probably thought he had said enough.

Chapter Twenty

Have you ever thought of doing your wedding flowers? If you have many hands, it's not as hard as you may think. What you do need is a plan, a refrigerator devoted to the flowers, a timeline of the work involved, and someone other than you, your bridal party, and family to execute the setup on the big day.

The next morning the wheels were still whirling in my brain. Was Clyde's ex-girlfriend, Maria Di'Rissi, being dismissed as a suspect in his death due to an ironclad alibi, or because she was the daughter of Mr. Di'Rissi? I pondered this as I sipped my black Americano in front of my kitchen fire. Yes, you heard that right. I had a fire going in the morning, and I was drinking my coffee…black. I had had a recent 'talking to' by my internist. He told me that I had two choices. I could go on high cholesterol medication, or I could do something about the amount of 'bad fat' I was consuming daily. Ouch. I wasn't so sure I loved coffee as much as I thought I did. Maybe it was the half and half I craved. But true story, my brain needed the caffeine. Maybe I'd switch to tea? The thought of putting anything in it (I know some people put milk in it), made me gag. I was trying to console myself with a fire. It wasn't helping my mood much.

I fired off a text to Brian.

Might as well get right to the point, is Maria Di'Rissi not a suspect in Clyde's murder because she's the daughter of a mobster

Brian: *Do you realize what you're accusing me of, Katie?*

Me: *Not YOU, Brian, just…*

Brian: *I AM the department, Kate* (yikes, he went the Kate route, he never called me 'Kate') *If you accuse the department, you accuse me*

Me: *Sorry, Bri. You're right.* I saw the bubbles working on the app, but then…nothing.

Well, I guess I got my answer. Now, I'm going to have to find out what Maria's alibi was. And I didn't think I'd get any help on the Brian front…for now. I tossed my phone in irritation.

Where did Ms. Di'Rissi hang out? I really wanted to talk to her. I had never seen her at Jen's, so that was out. I knew someone who might know. I pulled my favorite cashmere throw over my legs and picked my phone up again.

Text to Sarah: *Where does Maria Di'Rissi hang out?*

Sarah: *Why?*

Me: *I want to talk to her*

Sarah: *Mistake*

Me: *I don't care*

Sarah: *Rooftop 100 most nights*

I guess it made sense. It was the hotspot in town for people a little younger than I, but older than the college crowd.

Me: *Let's go tonight*

Sarah—*Laughing emoji*

Me: *I'm going, hope you come with me. I need you.* Did I really just say I needed Sarah Deloro? Well…I do.

Sarah: *Fiiiiiiinnnnne Be ready at 10:00. I'll drive*

Me: *At night????*

Sarah: *Katie…*

Dang! How invested in this plan was I? That was bedtime. Sure, I investigated after dark, but it was dark by 6:00 this time of year.

Now to the more pressing issue, what was I going to wear? I'm not sure I had anything in my closet that would work. And I don't think Rooftop 100 was the type of place I could wear my daily uniform of khakis, a sweater set, and my pearls. I had lost a few pounds, and I was a smaller woman (read shorter) than Ellis…maybe I could raid her closet? Would I have to ask? If

I did, she'd accuse me of stretching her clothes out which would be true. But what other choice did I have? Wait…I had that pair of pleather pants I bought for twelve dollars from Ann Taylor at last year's holiday sale. I had no use for them and had never worn them, but I couldn't resist a deal of twelve dollars…Silly, I know. Would they fit? As I remember, they had been super tight when I tried them on a year ago.

I flew to my closet, rummaged around, and finally located the pleather pants. I'd have to do something about this closet disaster soon. I snorted, yeah, right. I pulled off my PJ bottoms and tried them on. They fit! I ran, tags bouncing against my waist to Ellis' closet. I slid hangers of tops to the left quickly in my frenzy. I finally pulled down a cropped sequined top with…a deep 'V.' Dare I show a little cleavage? What the heck. You can bet Sarah Deloro would. While I couldn't hang with her epic proportions, I could hold my own. I slipped the top on, perfect, even if I'd have to find a different bra that could accommodate the 'cleavage.'

I looked at my bare feet. Shoot. I needed shoes, something other than my daily Allbirds or penny loafers. I bent down and dug through the floor that made Ellis' closet. Yuck. I'd have to do something about this closet, too. And then I found them, the perfect platform sandals. I looked at my bare feet. A pedicure was definitely in order. I'd do it myself and then slapped a quick dinner together for Ellis. She had volleyball practice and would be hungry when she got home. I was going to take a nap now; I kid you not. If I was going to stay up so late, I needed it and lots of, gag, coffee.

The hard part of the night would be getting out of the house in my clubbing get-up without Ellis seeing. She would make fun of me, and for sure not be happy with me borrowing her shoes and top. But what she didn't know wouldn't hurt her. I'm sure she had thought that about me.

Turns out I didn't have to worry much. Ellis came home, grumpy, showered, ate the chicken salad I had made, and announced she was on her way to her room to do the mountain of homework her sadistic teachers had piled on her. She didn't even ask for Kevin, her boyfriend, to come over to study.

Sarah was right on time. She flashed her brights from the driveway. I grabbed a North Face fleece, my crossbody bag, and headed out to meet her. I'd text Ellis from the car that I had a last-minute errand to do.

Sarah looked me over from head to toe as I entered her plush Range Rover.

"Looking pretty swanky, Manet. Where'd you get that 'fit'?" I couldn't tell by her tone if she was condescending or impressed.

I looked at her skin-tight jeans and cream sleeveless silk blouse, showing A LOT of cleavage, and sighed. "Where'd you get yours?" She looked fantastic, of course, she did.

We were stopped at a stop sign, and she turned to me, her face an eerie blue with the instrument lights glowing back at her. "Not bad, Katie, not bad," she said appraising me. "I find it hard to believe that you had all that in your closet, Mrs. Cleaver." She referenced the mom in the old black and white sitcom, "Leave it to Beaver." We were too young to have watched the show, but we both knew of it.

"Ha ha," I shot back. Good one, Katie, I thought. Jeeze.

"Get your club outfit from your kid?" She continued to taunt me.

"As a matter of fact, I had the pants already."

"That's a fact," was all she said, then concentrating on driving.

When we were almost there, Sarah decided to give me a tutorial. "You know who owns this joint, right, Katie?"

"Ah, no," I muttered. "How would I know that, Ms. Real Estate?"

"Has nothing to do with real estate, Katie. Everyone knows who owns Rooftop 100."

"Are you going to enlighten me?" Why did she have to be such a pain in the butt?

It was only a five-minute drive to 'Rooftop 100,' I could see already that parking would be an issue. It was a Monday night, for God's sake. Who *were* these people? There was a whole other world in my small town that, up until now, I knew nothing about. Sarah valeted as if she knew the ropes, and I imagine she did. She was young, well, young-ish, and single. And fairly pretty, okay, she was stunning.

We entered the foyer for the restaurant/bar and took the elevator up to 'Rooftop 100.' When the elevator doors opened, my senses were assaulted with loud music, flashing lights and the, if not good food, spicy food. Wow!

We were greeted by a hostess, and I all of a sudden had the fear that we were going to have to wait behind a velvet rope. Sarah smiled at the slim hostess, and she smiled back. Sarah took the lead, and we wound our way around the club/restaurant/bar looking for a place to light. It appeared the club was circular, for I surely felt like I was walking in circles. Finally, we saw a couple of open oversized chairs that appeared out of the way. We could still see the massive bar and the dance floor, but we weren't in the thick of things. Wait…was that my doctor over there dancing with some sweet young thing? Gross! Oh my God, there was my banker? And he was dancing with another guy. Who knew? I'm not sure this was my vibe, but I bet I could get a lot of business hanging out here—but then did these people look like the marrying kind?

A server came over to take our drink orders. Could her skirt be any shorter? I sounded in my head just like the middle-aged mom that I was. I ordered a sparkling water, and Sarah a chardonnay. We watched the dancers for a while, and two men came up and asked us to dance. I was dumbstruck, but Sarah declined for us graciously.

"Might not be a bad idea for us to dance," I whispered to Sarah.

"Always better to be the observer. Look," she indicated with her chin, "orange top, and blue jeans, white sandals," (white sandals! OMG!!) "that's Maria Di'Rissi."

She was a good dancer; she made her body move in ways I could only imagine. She wasn't a looker, though, but she had nice hair and good skin.

I looked at her and just knew she wasn't going to talk to me. I needed her phone.

"I need her phone, Sarah." I turned my gaze from the dancefloor and looked Sarah square in the eye.

Sarah was taking the first sip of her wine which had just been delivered by our server. She swallowed wrong and started choking.

I went into 'mom' mode. "Can you breathe? Can you talk? Shall I hit you on the back?"

Sarah shook her head as she continued coughing. She finally got out,

"You'd love that, wouldn't you Manet?" She rasped out. Her eyes watered, and tears threatened to run down her cheeks. She dabbed her eyes with her sleeves. Then patted her chest as her breathing returned to almost normal.

"Oh, my God, Katie! Are you crazier than you look? You can't take Maria Di'Rissi's phone. How would you even get it?

"I don't know, but I do know all our secrets are in our phones. And I need to see hers. It's for Addalee," I wheedled.

Sarah stood up. I'm out. You can come with me now, or uber home. But I want no part of this. You're crazy even thinking of stealing the phone of a mob boss's daughter." She looked a combination of scared and impressed.

"Coming?" She challenged.

"No," I answered. I could be stubborn, too.

She shook her head at me, her gorgeous dangling pearl and diamond earrings dancing against her long neck as she did so. I would love to be able to wear such long dangling earrings, but they wouldn't flatter short, old me. Yup, still hated her.

I didn't think she would, but she picked up her cashmere wrap and headed for the door without a backward glance at me. I imagine she thought I'd be scurrying behind her, but I held firm.

I watched Maria at the bar for several minutes and finally got the courage to approach the bar when a seat next to her opened up. A man next to her kissed her cheek and bade her goodnight. I slowly, nonchalantly made my way to the long bar, set with barstools with conformable looking backs. An open seat appeared to be rare, and the fact that one opened right next to Maria had to be a good sign, right? I took a deep breath and wished I had had a drink with Sarah when one was offered to me for courage. I noticed that Maria was drinking a dirty martini with three olives; I would order the same and did so when a bartender appeared almost instantly. She was cute, a redheaded, and didn't seem to be a day older than Ellis.

I readied my big mom purse on my lap and smiled when the bartender presented me with my cocktail.

"Shall I start a tab?" She asked?

"No, just this one for me," I smiled back. I'd like the check, so I don't have to bother you when I'm ready to head out. She came right back with my bill, and I paid her in cash. I had been watching and knew where the restaurant's cameras were, at least the visible ones. I tried to avert my face from their view. Sarah underestimated me. I wasn't going to rush this; it was a two-step process. I sat and sipped, watching the level of Maria's glass and olive consumption. She ate one, I ate one. She sipped; I sipped. Then, my probably one and only opportunity opened up. Someone came around the corner of the circular space and Maria's group was pleased and surprised. They yelled, they whooped, they embraced. I quickly switched our glasses, careful to hold Maria's glass by the stem. I sat for a few more moments, waiting to make sure no one called me out (not sure what I'd do if they did) and until my sweet bartender was called away down the bar. Then I reached into my mom bag, grabbed a gallon-sized Ziploc bag, and opened it. Did I mention I'm a wedding planner? Ha ha. I carry anything you'd ever want in my pocketbook. I leaned over and poured the remaining martini into the drain tray of the bar and slid the glass into my bag. It's important you do not look around as you do something sneaky. That is a dead giveaway. So, if someone saw me, I wouldn't know. I sat another minute, then rose to go, but not before I left a ten-dollar bill tip for my sweet bartender. We service people had to stick together. I went to the elevator, got in—no one stopped me, thank God.

When the elevator doors opened into the foyer, who was standing there tapping her foot impatiently but…Sarah Deloro.

"Thought you left," I said, less friendly than I should have. She had waited for me, after all.

"Well, aren't you a peach," she fired back. "Let's go. We can bicker in the car, safer there." She grabbed my arm and pulled me along. I switched my pocketbook to the other arm. Had to take care of that precious cargo.

Sarah handed the valet her claim ticket, and her car was brought around in seconds. She had probably slid the valet a nice little tip when she parked to have it ready when we needed it. She tipped the young man, and we both climbed into the SUV.

"Did anything happen?"

Her lack of faith in my skills annoyed me. I didn't answer. Was I being childish, yeah, a little.

"Spill, Manet. What happened?" Better choice of words. Of course, something happened

"Did you get her phone?" She peppered me as she looked over.

"Eyes on the road, Deloro."

"Yes, Mom," she sing-songed.

"No, I didn't get her phone. That was never the plan."

"But you said…"

I cut her off. "Of course I want her phone, but I have to do some prep work first."

Sarah took her hand off the wheel and gave me a 'come on' gesture.

"Well, even if I got the phone, surely, she would have some sort of security on it. So, I saw this thing on a cop show where they took a fingerprint off a glass, put it on some tape, and used that to get into someone's phone."

"Oh my God, Katie, that's the most stupid thing I've ever heard, or…it's the most brilliant?"

"I know, I'm not sure on which side of the fence I fall on this one. Let's go to my house, and we'll try it out."

All the lights, save for one in the kitchen, were out. My sweet daughter, thinking of me. I had texted her when Sarah and I had pulled out of the driveway on our way to Rooftop that I had an errand to run and might be late. Thank goodness she didn't quiz me. I didn't want to lie to her, and sure didn't want to say I was going to the Rooftop. Ellis's room was dark, please God, don't let her wake and come down to her mother pulling a stolen glass out of her pocketbook and trying to pull fingerprints from it.

We set up in the kitchen where the light was the best. I made us each an Americano. I knew that I'd pay with a restless night's sleep for that indulgence, but I wasn't sure I'd be awake or sharp enough for the task at hand if I didn't drink it.

We sipped our Americanos, and then I brought out the precious cargo—the martini glass. I placed it front and center on the kitchen island, still safe in its Ziplock bag.

We both walked around it, not sure really what I was looking for, can't say what Sarah was thinking.

"Have to say I'm impressed that you walked off with this, and no one came running after you, either a bartender or one of Mr. Di'Rissi's henchmen." That made me shiver. What had I done? And was I brave enough to follow through, if…my harebrained scheme worked?

I put on some latex gloves that I had left over from Covid and opened the bag. I once again held the glass by the stem. I held the glass up to the light. It was riddled with smudges and fingerprints.

I'm sure my process was clumsy and inept, but after a quick Google search, I found the best way to transfer fingerprints on a glass to another surface, which *technically* should allow me to use that surface to open Maria's phone if she used the fingerprint option. I knew I was putting a lot of weight on the chance she did this, but what other option did I have? I'd never be able to guess her password. I might be able to use a photo of her the way I had done to open a phone last spring (yes, a phone that wasn't mine) and I always could try that if the fingerprint option didn't work.

"Can you grab a photo of Maria somewhere, from one of her socials, or whatnot, in case this fingerprint deal doesn't work?"

"On it," and Sarah went about grabbing a picture of Maria from her Instagram. She printed it on my laser printer. I followed the google search instructions and with Sarah's help, completed the process. I'd find out tomorrow night if it worked or not.

"Well, I need a drink now, Manet. The stress of that was nasty. I have the shakes from all the detail work." She wasn't kidding; she held her hands up, and they were trembling. It was the adrenaline.

It was after 2:00 AM. "You can drink all you want, as long as you stay the night, Sarah. We're too tired, and it's too late to mix alcohol and fatigue."

"Okay, Mom, let's have that drink."

* * *

When I woke up the next morning, Sarah was gone, but there was a note.

What time tonight, Manet?

Thank God, I was worried I'd have to do this on my own, and I wasn't sure I could.

Chapter Twenty-one

We were back at the scene of last night's crime. No one barred my entrance; the bartender, the same woman as last night, didn't look at me funny. I think I'd gotten away with stealing the martini glass.

Tonight, Sarah was dressed much the same as she had been last night, only a different colored silk shell; tonight, pale, pale blue. I had copied her look a little, wearing a pair of Ellis's jeans…okay, not her exact size jeans, but ones I had bought in a size too large for her and had never returned. They were still snug…okay, *very* snug. I had paired them with a cream silk blouse, but chose long sleeves. My upper arms weren't as toned as Sarah's, and I needed the coverage.

Maria was holding court again. I guess she wasn't grieving too hard for poor Clyde. Either that, or she was drowning her sorrow in booze.

It was about 10:00 PM, and Sarah had suggested we wait until they had a little more to drink before we made a move. I felt an unwelcome dampness under my arms. Really? I was getting sweaty *now*.

I ordered a glass of the chardonnay tonight; I needed some liquid reinforcement. Sarah almost guzzled hers. I think this was the first time I have ever seen Sarah Deloro nervous. Well, I was too, but not as shaky as

Sarah. Who was the smarter woman? I'd have to say Sarah. I should be more fearful of Maria and her father.

Based on last night, I noticed that Maria liked her phone close by. She had left it on the bar the entire time I had watched her, and then sat next to her. I was planning on the same behavior tonight. It was my only chance. It wasn't as if I could grab her bag and dig through it.

Our plan was simple. I was going to wait for, hopefully, a seat to open near her, and Sarah was going to go say 'Hello.' I would then throw a napkin over her phone and grab it off the bar. Off to the ladies I would go with Maria's fingerprint. I had the photo Sarah had printed of Maria for backup. I would then attempt to open her phone. The plan was unlikely to work, I do know. Sarah had given me seven minutes to look at her texts and emails, as well as her browser history. Then, I would slide in and…return the phone! Easy peasy, right? Oh my gosh, there were so many things that could go wrong, including my own personal safety. I refused to think about what this act could mean for Ellis. Just the thought made me rethink the whole thing. All that could go wrong was that Maria would look for her phone and not find it immediately. I could then 'find' it on the bar floor. Right? RIGHT?? I asked myself.

"Let's do this." Sarah stood up, squaring her shoulders. She fluffed her hair, adjusted her silk shell, then said, "Game time, Manet."

A seat opened up two away from Maria, but a very skinny girl tried to beat me to it. I pretended I didn't notice her and bumped her (gently!). My superior weight knocked her off kilter, balanced as she was on her ridiculously high heels. Nabbed the seat, yay me!

"Sorry!" I mouthed to her rather condescendingly, as I adjusted myself on the barstool and gave her my mom smile. She sulked off.

I gave Sarah a nod, then watched her walk into the group surrounding Maria; she was greeted warmly. There were hugs and air kisses all around. They had just seen her last night! Dang it all. No one was moving. Then Sarah worked her magic and asked the man seated next to Maria a question. He feigned not being about to hear, and he left his stool to go to her side. This was my moment. I checked for Maria's phone, as I couldn't put eyes on it with that guy sitting next to her. It was there. I could do this. Yes, yes, I could.

I hopped over and took the empty bar stool next to Maria. The cute little bartender noticed and came to take my drink order. "Dirty martini, three olives, right?" She smiled. I smiled back. Shoot, she remembered me.

"Right," I affirmed. She went right to mixing my cocktail, and in a flash, she was back with it.

"Tab, or check?"

"Check," I said, and she whipped it out of her pocket (she was good!). I paid—cash, of course. I left a generous tip, and then, I did what I advise against. I looked around. I waited a couple of beats, and then a couple more. I put a cloth napkin I had brought from home over Maria's phone, which rested on the bar just like last night. The napkins matched the ones at the club—(I had noticed the color and brand last night), there are so many advantages to being a wedding planner. I let the napkin wrapped phone sit for a moment, then I swooped it up a fluid motion and sauntered in the direction of the ladies' room. I was poised for a hand to tap me on the shoulder to ask what the heck I was doing. But it didn't happen. As I turned the corner to enter the ladies, I did take a look over my shoulder. Maria had made like she was going to turn to where her phone had been on the bar, but Sarah leaned in and embraced her, put her hands on Maria's upper arms in an extra 'warm' greeting. Sarah's smile was big. Maria responded in kind. They started chatting animatedly.

Maria had been ready to check her phone. I had maybe five minutes, eight tops. I wasn't sure I could get much done. What if she looked for her phone and couldn't find it? That gave me another three to four minutes, but also raised the bar of the chance of getting caught.

The ladies' room had two stalls. They were both empty, and I hoped they would stay that way. The last thing I needed was a line.

I dug in my pocketbook and pulled out ten sheets of paper towels. I placed them on the toilet seat and sat down, yuck. I then pulled out the 'fingerprint' I had on a piece of plastic. I woke up Maria's phone, and it asked for a fingerprint or a password. Now, to hope that I had the right fingerprint, and more than that…it worked. Oh…my…God, it worked! My hands shook. I never really thought it would, if I was going to be honest. I was very glad Maria had an iPhone. I was able to navigate it. It would have taken me a lot longer to figure out the different operating system of an android—time I didn't have.

Two women came in. Okay, here it started.

"Oh, crap, someone's in one stall." One slurred.

"Well, I'll go first, I really gotta go. Then you go," voice number one dictated.

"Fiiiiine voice number two, the more drunken one, replied." I could hear her opening and closing her pocketbook, probably reapplying lipstick.

I opened Maria's message app and typed in Clyde's name. Yay! She hadn't erased his contact info. There was a whole string of texts, as you could imagine. I went back a couple of weeks. This was good. If he was going to message his girlfriend, or ex-girlfriend, anything important, it would have been fairly recently—close to his death.

Baby, I love you, you have to believe me. It was just a mistake with Aubry, you know she has no standards, ha ha. Please let it go. I have some good news. Clyde had written.

You know I hate her. Why would you cheat on me with her?

Baby it was a mistake. Don't you want to hear my news. If it all works out, I can get you that house on the Cape you want.

Maria answered. *Seriously? Must be some big news!*

I have some real stuff on him now and I can leverage that into cash.

How did that happen? And how do you know he won't tell my father?

He won't tell your dad, because it shows that he's cheating him, and we all know how your father deals with that.

Gulp. Yikes. Who was Clyde talking about? I looked through the rest of the thread, but a name was never mentioned. They changed the subject, got a little graphic about the personal side, and I closed the app.

Then *my* phone buzzed with a text alert. Come back NOW!

I returned Maria's phone to the home screen, which is where it was when I opened it, clicked it off, stashed it in my pocketbook, put my own phone away, and flushed the toilet.

I exited the stall and washed my hands. The waiting woman glared at me. I smiled. She waddled to the stall with a little hop to her step. I guess she was entitled to that glare. Some things can't wait.

I left the ladies and sauntered to my seat at the bar, saved, I hoped, by draping my sweater over the barstool back. Yep, saved. I'm sure Sarah wouldn't let anyone sit there anyway. I met her eyes, she bugged hers out at me in some sort of warning, I guess. I sat down on my barstool, reached into my bag, placed the napkin over Maria's phone, and pulled it out. I really should have had the phone covered before—but I'm not perfect. I turned my body away, and as planned, I did so. Sarah moseyed over and 'brushed' the napkin to the floor with her arm, revealing the phone, as she said, 'hello' to me and gave me an air kiss. She whispered in my ear, "She never missed it. Productive?"

I gave a quick nod.

"Let's get out of here." She started walking toward the exit.

I double-stepped to catch up with her. "Aren't you going to say 'Good-bye' to your friends?"

Sarah looked over her shoulder at me and rolled her eyes. "They're so drunk, they won't notice I'm gone." I wasn't so sure, but I shrugged and followed her to the elevator.

Once we had claimed her Range Rover from the valet and were all buckled in, we were on our way. She turned to me with expectation. I wish she would stop doing that while she drove.

"Well?" Sarah queried.

"According to a text thread between Clyde and Maria, he had cheated on her, and she was mad. He was trying to get her back with the promise of a house on the Cape. She wanted to know how he could afford that…he was blackmailing someone. My guess is that someone was the killer."

"Good info, but not enough, obviously." Did she just sneer at me? It felt like it. I tamped down my natural inclination to make excuses or apologize. "So, what's next, Sherlock?" Sarah continued.

We had just pulled up to my house. "I don't know yet, let me sleep on it We can meet tomorrow morning at Jen's at 8:00. Or is that too early for you?" I said as I assertively shut her door.

"No 'thank you'?" I heard her muffled reply.

That Sarah Deloro. I mouthed, "Thanks." But I smiled.

Chapter Twenty-two

Grooms: will you wear a suit, a blazer and slacks or a tux? Will you wear just a shirt and suspenders (for a more casual look)? Whatever you choose, don't leave it until last minute. Your attire is important and sets a tone. But if you plan to rent something, think long and hard about it. You just may pay the same to buy as rent, and if you buy, you have a suit to keep.

The next morning found me seated at Jen's table at The Perk with Jen and Sarah. We had brought Jen up to speed, and she was frankly horrified at our antics. I was glad I didn't ask her to join. I think I would have been a little hurt if she outright rejected me. I knew on some sort of level that I was behaving irresponsibly, but there was a reason for it (Addalee) and I don't think I really appreciated Jen's censure. But was that the only reason? Had I really not gotten over her betrayal of me back in high school? Of course, she had apologized, and I had, rather graciously, in my opinion, accepted. But had I fully forgiven her? I shut down that thought. Nothing good would come from chasing that.

"You're lucky to get out of that situation without anyone being the wiser," Jen scolded, crossing her arms over her torso. Sarah and I traded covert glances. "It all could have gone so wrong." Jen shook her head, her face flushing.

"I thought it was the most fun I've had in years." Sarah chimed in.

"More fun than last spring when you two were running all over doing much the same thing?" Jen asked, judgment in her voice.

"That was to help *you*, Jen," I reminded her.

Jen looked down at the ceramic mug printed with 'The Perk' on it. "I know," she said softly, "and I really appreciate it, but that doesn't mean I don't worry about your reckless behavior."

Is that how I was acting? With recklessness? I hoped not. I had too much on the line. Maybe Jen was right. I was a mother, a business owner. But then I thought about Addalee's sweet face, and the fact that she was so innocent. I had to prove that.

"I have to get back to work," Jen said, rising, taking her mug with her, then smoothing her work apron with her free hand. "Just be careful, okay?" Worry creased her brow.

Both Sarah and I gave her a nod but were silent. I would promise Jen nothing. Maybe she was a little jealous of my budding friendship with Sarah? She needn't be. We were good partners, but would never, could never, be close friends. One had to trust someone to be that, and I don't think I totally trusted her. Just think what she had done last spring, throwing me under the bus with that developer. We did have a closer, unspoken relationship since the situation with the Doc and his health, however.

"So, what are we going to do, Manet?" Sarah asked. She really *was* a good partner, though.

"We have to talk to Maria. We have to find out who Clyde was blackmailing. I thought we could avoid that by breaking into her phone, but we just can't."

Sarah blew out a big breath, ruffling her bangs. "And where is Addalee in this whole scenario. It seems we are doing all the risky work. And messing with Maria and questioning her *is* risky, Katie, don't deceive yourself." As if to accentuate this, she took a big gulp of her latte, for sure cold now, as if it were a tequila shot.

"You know Addie. She's wringing her hands, crying, and now, fighting with Cory and her mother-in-law. Now with the baby on the way, I don't think she can take the added stress.

"We always did coddle her. At some point, she is going to have to stand up for herself." Sarah looked at me squarely.

"Agreed, but just not right now. So, when can we talk to Maria?

All the bravado in the world wouldn't cover for the nervousness I was experiencing as Sarah and I waited for Maria Di'Rissi to open her front door. I can't really believe that Sarah got us an audience with her.

Maria Di'Rissi lived in the new condos built last year in Eastbury which catered to the upper crust empty nesters, or a singleton like Maria. Those folks had funds to burn, wanted a splashy place to live with all the amenities, but didn't want to worry about maintenance or a lawn. I had never been here before, but was duly impressed with the elegance of the property and the lushness of the landscaping.

When you entered the gated community, you were almost overcome with the beauty of the grounds. Granted, it was fall in New England, so how could it *not* be beautiful, but it was apparent that no cost had been spared to maintain the gardens and landscaping in pristine condition.

We drove around until we found Maria's building address and parked in a visitor's spot. Her unit was 'B', which faced the back of the building, and as it turns out, a small gem of a lake. I'd have to check a town map, but I'm pretty sure that lake was man-made. It had a dock, with a few canoes pulled up to shore and lots of Adirondack chairs scattered around the lake's beach. Wow, did I make a mistake buying my historic home? This seemed the way to go! But Ellis deserved a house with a yard and all the perks. Even if it meant I had to shovel the driveway and the sidewalk a time or two in the winter.

We knocked to no answer. I was beginning to wonder if Maria was home, or if she was plain avoiding Sarah, when she answered her door with a flourish. When I was standing face to face with her, I realized she was even shorter than I thought. I am not a tall woman at five-foot-four, but I towered over her. And Sarah looked like a giant as she embraced her in a condolence visit hug—at least that was our story.

"You poor darling," Sarah cooed. She rocked the stubby Maria back and forth. They ended the embrace, Maria's heavily made-up face threatening to smear with the tears I saw in her eyes. It looked as if she had been a victim of some nasty acne as a teen and used her makeup almost as a mask. I knew from some friends how debilitating that condition could be. She had my sympathy.

"This is my dear friend, Kate Ludlow. She worked with Clyde, and when she heard I was coming by, she wanted to join me to offer her condolences too. I know we said hello at the Rooftop, but that just doesn't seem enough, you know." Sarah finished.

Maria nodded as her gaze shifted to me, and I got the chills. I thought of that old phrase, 'I felt like someone walked on my grave.' That.

"Nice to meet you, Maria. I'm sorry, though, that we have to meet under these circumstances." I offered her a freshly defrosted pound cake I kept in my freezer for events such as this, or a bake sale for one of Ellis' sports teams.

Maria looked at my offering, and I *swear* she turned up her nose, but it was so fleeting, I then second-guessed myself. Her smile brightened when Sarah presented her with her offering, a gorgeous bouquet of pink hydrangeas

"Come in, please," Maria opened her door wider, and we were treated to the most beautiful entry and living room filled with light and sunshine. The opposite wall was all windows with a golden view of the lake. Whoever said that the sunlight in a New England fall was more yellow, more gold, than summer was correct. This day proved it. We followed Maria into her living room, which was furnished with separate pieces that all worked well together. She did have one loveseat, but the rest of the furnishings were composed of individual armchairs in varying colors and fabrics.

"Sit anywhere. I'm going to put this...down," she looked at my bundt cake with almost a quizzical air, "and I'll get us some coffee, unless you'd like tea?"

I wanted neither, but didn't want to say no to this scary woman. Not sure how she'd react.

"Coffee would be great," Sarah and I said together. We really were spending too much time together.

Sarah chose a pale blue chair, and I chose a green one. They both faced the lake.

Maria was bustling around the kitchen, which was open to the living room. The kitchen counters were a lovely cream marble, and the cabinets were painted a light green. I loved the farm sink that was featured in the kitchen. I've always wanted one.

In the blink of an eye, Maria brought a tray over to us that had a China coffee pot, mugs, and a cream/sugar set that had a 'Pottery Barn" ceramic vibe. There were also little cookies that were so often featured in Italian bakeries. While I adored sweets, these cookies were not my jam. I wasn't a fan of the ever-present almond flavor.

I took two when she offered them to me, though. I wasn't going to have her hate me over a couple of cookies.

Sarah took the lead. "How are you holding up, honey?" she asked Maria… 'honey'?

Maria put her own coffee cup down next to the tray, on her eyes welled up again.

"I just wish we had been on better terms before he passed. If I had known…"

"Oh, Honey, how could you know? What was going on? What were you two on the outs about?" I thought Sarah was going too far, too quickly, but Maria seemed to want to bare her soul, and didn't seem to care that someone she had just met was there listening. Maybe she liked that component.

"Well," Maria started, drawling out the 'well.' Her whole facial expression changed. She looked ready to have a good gossip. Like she was talking about someone else, not herself. " You know Aubrey Lucca, right?"

I didn't know an Aubrey Lucca, but that didn't mean Sarah didn't.

"Sure, cocktail waitress at Starlight, right?"

Maria nodded and scooted to the end of her seat. "She and Clyde were having a thing, right under my nose. And she was my best friend since pre-K!" Now she looked outraged. "I'm not sure who I'm madder at, Aubrey or Clyde." She caught herself, well, obviously Aubrey…now." Maria dug her hands through her luxurious dark brown hair. Her eyebrows may be overgrown, and her skin over-made-up, but her hair, her hair was to die for. It was just gorgeous. It was shiny, and the curls were most definitely natural and just right.

"I never liked her," Sarah said with venom. I felt like I was watching a soap opera. My eyes went from Sarah to Maria as they went back and forth, hating on Aubrey.

"I know, right?!?" Maria responded. "Oh, I've missed you, Sarah. I let all my good friends drop when I was all caught up with Clyde. Well, no more!"

CHAPTER TWENTY-TWO

"Did you two break up over her?" Sarah asked.

"You bet we did! I won't deal with a cheater." Well, we had that in common, Maria, I thought. Me either.

"Did you ever think about forgiving him? Did he ever try to get you back? You're such a catch; I can't see him letting you go easily." Sarah gushed as Maria preened, twisting a curl round and round her thick index finger.

"Oh, he tried. Tried to woo me with the promise of a house on the Cape. He knew that my dad would get me one, but I wanted my man to get it for me. But the way he was going to get the money for it, I just didn't like it." Maybe Maria had some scruples, maybe she was better than her gangster father and was above blackmail.

"Sounds mysterious, kinda dark," Sarah made her eyes big. She was borderline going too far with her leading questions.

Maria's cell began scooting across the coffee table as it vibrated with an incoming call. She picked it up to stop its progression, but frowned when she read it.

"Sorry, guys, I have to take this." Maria left the room; I'm guessing for her bedroom.

"Laying it on a little thick, don't ya think, Sarah?" I hissed at her. "Keep it up, and she'll know you have an agenda!"

"You don't know these people, Katie!" she hissed back. "You can't be too subtle with them. You asked me to do this, LET ME DO IT!" She whisper-yelled.

I leaned back in my chair, properly chastened. Maria came stomping back in and went straight to her coat closet. She grabbed a beautiful suede and shearling coat, a type I have long coveted.

"So sorry, guys, but that was an emergency phone call. I have to head out."

"Oh, no worries, Maria, I hope everything is okay," Sarah almost baby-talked. Gag.

Maria gave us the bum rush, and we were out the door in a flash.

Maria gave Sarah an air kiss and bade me farewell as well. "Nice to meet you, Kathy," she said. And she didn't even thank me for the delicious bundt cake, ha ha.

I almost replied, 'It was nice to meet you, too, Melissa.' But I refrained. She wasn't someone I wanted for a friend, so what the heck.

"Let's go, Kathy," Sarah wheedled as we climbed into her SUV, then she cackled.

Chapter Twenty-three

This isn't a new idea, but it is a good one. Consider a card in either your mailed invitation packet or space on your e-invite for your guests to request dance songs. There's nothing that can get your guests up and dancing than playing songs that resonate with the dancers.

So, the whole thing with Maria was a bust. I don't think we gathered any intel from that visit. Sarah and I drove off in silence. I was miffed and not above taking it out on poor Sarah.

"Well, that was a giant waste of time," I groused.

"Not entirely," she responded. What? My mind whirled with questions.

I turned in my seat toward her. "What gives, Sarah?"

"Look in my pocketbook."

I reached back behind Sarah's seat and pulled up her Louis. I opened it and pulled out of a thick cream colored envelope with the name, 'Maria' on the outside.

"Open it."

My hands shook a little, but I opened it and withdrew a beautifully engraved…wedding invitation. I looked at the elaborate printing. It was an invitation to Maria for Clyde's sister's wedding. It made sense. She was Clyde's sister, and Maria had been Clyde's girlfriend, although an ex at the time of his death.

I held the invitation up. "And what am I supposed to do with this?" I'm sure the irritation was apparent in my voice.

"Well, go, silly!" Sarah smirked.

It was my turn to smirk. "Yeah, right. Begging you to take me as your plus one to a wedding that you're invited to is one thing. Completely crashing a wedding is another."

"I didn't realize you were such a baby, Manet."

Oh, that Sarah knew exactly what she was doing. Okay then, challenge accepted. Somehow, I knew she wouldn't be my date. Okay, Brian. You're on, I thought.

Chapter Twenty-four

So, you think you can do it all? You can't. You can do a lot of DIY decorating if you have lots of hands, but you can't do it all. On your wedding day, your family and guests will want to also dress for the day, take photos, enjoy. So, hire some tasks out.

Ellis was at an away volleyball game, and a face-to-face meeting in my office with a bride prevented me from going. I hated to miss her games. But this is the life of a working mother. I did my best to schedule work around her calendar, but sometimes it couldn't be done. Grant was back on the support schedule, so I was thankful for that. He had even reimbursed me for his missed back payments. The hateful Heather, the woman he cheated on me with, our next-door neighbor, was a money suck. Grant was much more liquid in the financial department since they had called it quits.

We were having an Indian Sumner—although the wording was perhaps not politically correct, it was an old term, and the definition was one last warm period of time before the chill of Fall arrived permanently. This time is so precious because everyone knows what is ahead: the stark, frigid weather of winter. I decided to walk to the office today, so that meant I had to walk home. But I would have made that choice anyway. The gentle breeze was soft on my bare shoulders, and I relished it.

Brian had finally agreed to accompany me to Sylvie's wedding. I knew he was a little suspicious as to why I would get an invite, but he let it go. I was racking my brain for a good wedding guest outfit. I just may have to go shopping again…uuuuggg.

Brian was working late tonight, but that was probably for the best. We had been off our normal relationship cadence since all the mishaps had been occurred with the reservations, and his missing suit from the dry cleaner. I almost felt as if he blamed me, which was ridiculous.

The trees were at their peak with their fall display. The reds, golds, oranges bursting upon the scene. This was many people's favorite time of year. It wasn't mine. There was too much of a melancholy vibe for me. I knew what was coming. I didn't hate winter; in fact, I rather liked it. But there was a barrenness to it that put me off. No, I preferred spring. Spring was the season of rebirth, new life. I was feeling all philosophical and thoughtful. I was in a particularly tree-covered part of my walk. It felt cozy and isolated. That was my excuse, anyway, for not hearing the thug sneak up on me. One minute, I was contemplating my favorite season, the next, I had a hand over my mouth and nose that reeked of cigarette smoke.

I froze, then began kicking wildly. The grip on my face grew more hostile. What the heck *were* those defensive moves I felt so confident I knew. Dang! I could remember nothing.

"I don't want to hurt you. But you can't get away, make it easy on yourself. This won't take long if you behave, and then I'll take you to your nice little house myself."

I stilled instantly in his hold. Should I go limp? I had heard that worked. I decided to comply…for now. I'd be strategic, wait for my chance. At least that is what I told myself to quell the panic rising in me. OH MY GOD! The perp walked me to a nearby vehicle, a blacked-out Suburban. Okay, at least my would-be rapist/kidnapper had some nice wheels. The door opened, and I was half lifted, half shoved into the backseat. There was someone else back there…it was Sarah!

It made me feel better to see her; misery loves company. And it also answered some questions. This must be about all the questions we were asking. It had to have something to do with Mr. Di'Rissi. Oh, God, maybe that was worse than some random dude grabbing me off the street.

I looked at Sarah, hoping she'd give me some reassurance. Our eyes met.

Sarah mouthed, "It's going to be okay." Did I feel better? I'm not sure, but I wasn't as scared.

We drove about half an hour, half of it off-road, if the rough ride was any indicator. Sarah and I were both more of less on the floor of the backseat, and that was fine with me. Harder to shoot me that way. The two men in the front told me that they had guns; I didn't need to see them to believe it. I heard one rack. The men were surprisingly quiet; I couldn't gather any information from their chit chat, there was none.

"Where are we going?" I whispered to Sarah, so glad they hadn't gagged us. I got merely a shoulder shrug. She didn't seem overly concerned. Maybe she was drunk, or drugged?

"That's it, up on the right," the passenger told the driver. The car slowed and made a right-hand turn onto what felt and sounded like gravel. The car came to a slow stop, and the driver cut the engine.

"Let's get these little ladies out and inside." The driver directed. He opened Sarah's door, and my guy opened mine. Like a double date, I thought with a hint of manic fear.

My guy had me up and out of the car before Sarah's had her and was marching me once more toward a structure that looked like a cabin. It was very dark out, but the sky, the little of it I could see between all the trees, was full of stars. We must be out in the country to have a sky like that. The cabin looked cozy and inviting, ha. I couldn't imagine a warm, fuzzy reception waiting for me.

My handler knocked twice on the cabin door, and a voice said, "Come." Friendly!

The door squeaked when he opened it, just like an old horror movie. Oh my God.

I would have been surprised if the man waiting for us had been any other than Mr. Di'Rissi. He was sitting in a rocking chair…smoking a tobacco pipe, like you'd see on the old TV 'Ozzie and Harriet.' I don't think he could have looked any more benign or grandfatherly. Especially when he smiled so matter-of-factly, as if he had not just kidnapped us. Would we press charges or report it to the police? Not if we wanted to live…IF they let us go. No plastic on the floor, so if they were going to kill us, they weren't going to do it here.

"Ladies, welcome," Mr. Di'Rissi's smile grew bigger. "Please, have a seat. He indicated a sofa adjacent to him, in front of the fireplace, which had a warm roaring fire.

Sarah and I gingerly sat on the sofa, turning simultaneously to face our captor. I sat on my hands, they were shaking so much.

"What can I offer you, coffee, tea, or perhaps something harder? I know this situation may have been unsettling…"

Ya think? I thought

"I'm fine, thanks," Sarah responded with a bit of snark.

What the heck. "I'd love an Irish whisky, neat," I said.

Mr. Di'Rissi laughed and snapped his fingers at someone behind him. "Nikko, Jamison's neat for Ms. Ludlow," he ordered.

Nikko brought my drink, and I accepted it gratefully and took a huge gulp, which made me cough. I quelched my little fit and enjoyed the warmth the whiskey spread through me. My hands were shaking less now.

"Ladies," Mr. Di'Rissi began, "I first have to apologize for the rather dramatic way I requested your presence here tonight." He smiled.

This suave, fatherly act was not going to work with me. I was mad as hell, now that I had stopped fearing for my life. How dare he? I think the whiskey was giving me courage that was probably misplaced. We were in real danger, and I wasn't as fearful as I should be. I opened my mouth to say something snarky. Sarah gave me a look, but I wasn't going to let it stop me. So, she pre-empted me.

"No hard feelings, Mr. Di'Rissi. But why are we here?"

Mr. Di'Rissi smiled at Sarah, but not with as much indulgence as before.

"I think you know the answer to that, Ms. Deloro.

Sarah and I looked at each other; I'm sure we couldn't keep the guilt from our eyes. We knew.

He walked around the chairs and in back of the loveseat, making, at least my anxiety soar. We didn't say anything, though. I think we decided by silent mutual agreement that we would wait for him to speak. Why feed him information he may not have?

"I understand you paid my darling daughter, Maria, a visit."

I glanced at Sarah without moving my head. I'd let her speak.

Sarah's face was white. She knew these people better than I did. The fact she was so worried finally put the fear of God into me. We had been kidnapped, and they let us see their faces. Either they didn't think we'd turn them in, or they were going to kill us.

Sarah finally found her voice. "Yes, we made a condolence call. We felt awful about poor Clyde. Any news on that front?"

Mr. Di'Rissi waved a finger at Sarah. "Sarah Deloro, you are a minx. You went on a fishing expedition. And I DON'T LIKE IT." Mr. Di'Rissi's voice boomed in the close quarters.

I could see the wheels turning in Sarah's head. She was going to cut her losses and 'fess up. But before she had the chance, I cut her off.

"Why did you grab us?" I avoided using the term 'kidnap, opened too many negative doors. I wanted him to think we would be fine with him if he just returned us home. And I, for one, would. I'd never say a word to anyone. I wasn't stupid, well, not much.

Now Mr. Di'Rissi's attention was turned to me. He turned his hard, blue-eyed gaze to me.

"Ah, Ms. Ludlow. You are a surprise in this scenario. I do not know much about you, but never fear my team is on it. You do have a lovely daughter, just like I do. We will do anything to protect our children, won't we, Ms. Ludlow?" His smile was slimy.

I half rose from my chair. How dare he mention Ellis? I felt my face flush. That whiskey was giving me a false bravado. Sarah put a calming…(or restraining?) hand on my arm. Mr. Di'Rissi gave a burst of genuine laughter, at least it seemed so to me. "Oh, Katie, may I call you Katie?"

I just nodded. "You're a little spitfire, aren't you? Your Ellis is safe. If I have issues with you," here he narrowed his eyes at me, "they will remain with you."

"Thank you," I managed. But I wouldn't let him off that easily. Not when my daughter was concerned. I would always stand up for her. "But just so we're clear," I used my mom voice, "If she is ever hurt, threatened, or just thinks someone is following her, I will come for you." Yes, my voice shook. I hope he didn't notice.

"Katie!" Sarah was horrified. "Do you know who you're talking to? Don't be stupid," she hissed to me quietly. Mr. Di'Rissi made a calm-down motion, pressing his palms down toward the floor.

"Do not be alarmed, Sarah, Ms. Ludlow, I hear you, but remember, respect is a very important thing." His eyes turned cold again. I couldn't push this man too far.

I conceded this. "Yes, sir," I replied. He gave me a small smile, then a stern look. I think we were good.

He changed tactics. "Now again, what do you know about Charlie and Clyde?" Sarah and I looked at each other. 'Charlie?' I thought and imagined Sarah did too.

"We don't know anything about Charlie," Sarah responded. I only know Clyde was going to photograph his and Remley's wedding."

Mr. Di'Rissi was silent. He looked first at Sarah and then at me. I was starting to sweat. And I should have let it go about Ellis. He said any issues would remain between us. Then I had to go shooting my mouth off. Oh my God. Perspiration was beading on my upper lip.

He stood up abruptly, startling both Sarah and me. Sarah actually recoiled a bit into her chair. "Well, ladies, that's about it for tonight. I'm sure I don't have to remind you that this was a friendly meeting between business associates. It would do no one any good to make more of this than it is. Understand?"

Both Sarah and I nodded. We were driven back to our homes, and that… was that. I knew I should feel greater fear, but somehow…I didn't. We all pick our battles, and I think that applied to Mr. Di'Rissi, too.

Chapter Twenty-five

Make sure you always have reserved signs on the first couple rows of your ceremony chairs or pews. The first two rows should always be kept open for family or perhaps the bridal party if the ceremony is a long religious one (the bridal party will be seated for their comfort). Perhaps the wedding party is over-large and there isn't ample room for them all to stand up front, another situation for the bridal party to be seated.

I awoke the next morning to sunlight streaming through my bedroom windows. What time was it? I raced downstairs to find a note from Ellis.

Mom, I know you were out late last night. I didn't want to wake you when I realized you weren't up—you're always up! I hope you have a good day. Love, E

PS Caught a ride with Kevin

Loved that kid. I dragged myself over to the espresso machine and started the arduous process of brewing the espresso for my Americano. It was worth it, though.

While I went on autopilot brewing the coffee, I thought about the bizarre business of last night. What kind of man thought he could grab two women off the street and expect them not to report him? Mr. Di'Rissi, that's who. And he was correct. I wouldn't speak of it—to anyone. But what I did know was that I had to talk to Charlie. Charlie had always been honest and upfront with me. He was a stand-up guy. He would explain all this away. I felt confident he would. I decided I'd call him and invite him over for coffee or lunch to go 'over wedding details' whenever he could fit me in. I knew he was busy; maybe it wouldn't even be today. I'd try, though. I'd feel better after we talked.

I fired off a text.

Have some details we should go over for the wedding, can you fit me in today or tomorrow, either for coffee or lunch? I'm working from home today.

How did I subtly say, 'And please don't bring Remley.' I still wasn't feeling forgiving.

I saw the bubbles on the text message floating.

Then, ***I can meet for coffee in about an hour. I'm working from home today, too.***

Charlie and I lived within walking distance of each other.

Perfect. See you in an hour.

Well, heck. I had to shower, dress, and figure out what I was going to serve. I couldn't just serve coffee. I went to the freezer. I had another pound cake frozen, this time lemon. I could slice it and nuke it if I had to. Done! My mouth watered. I sure liked my own baking.

I ran up the stairs and jumped in the shower. First task completed, I went to my closet to decide what to wear. Today called for leggings and a grey cashmere pencil skirt. I paired it with a white t-shirt and a black, cropped cashmere sweater. I slipped on a pair of AllBird flats and…done! I looked at my face in the dresser mirror as I left my room, and backtracked. I needed a little help in the hair and makeup department. So, I smoothed my dark brown hair down and put a grey headband on that matched my skirt and applied some tinted moisturizer, lip gloss, and mascara. A quick glance in the mirror confirmed I looked better.

I raced down the stairs, grateful every time I did so that my injured leg was so much better.

I had just entered the foyer when my doorbell rang. Charlie was prompt.

I opened the door to another gorgeous bouquet of flowers, this time yellow mums.

"I came alone, didn't think you were ready for a dose of Remley yet," he smiled wryly before I ushered him in. I didn't respond. What could I say?

I took the flowers and waved my hand to him in a beckoning motion. We went into my large kitchen; I had a fire ready to go in the fireplace and bent down and threw a match onto the kindling, then grabbed a vase to put the flowers in water. I even added some flower food.

"Let's sit in front of the fire," I invited. Charlie sat down on one of the wicker padded chairs. "I'll get our coffee. I brought a tray over with mugs, cream and sugar, dessert plates, napkins, and…slices of the lemon pound cake, which turned out surprisingly well after I nuked it. Of course, I had to taste-test.

Charlie held out his mug for me to fill from my coffee server and accepted a dessert plate with the cake already on it.

"Cream, sugar?" I asked.

"Black is great." I should have known that.

Charlie took a bite of cake and made a happy face. "Delicious, Katie."

I smiled my thanks. "Charlie," I started, this was awkward. He raised his eyebrows, as if to say, 'yes, go on.' I was so uncomfortable; how did I do this?

"Charlie, did you have some sort of other relationship with Clyde, other than just having him be your wedding photographer?"

Charlie looked uncomfortable, then smiled that good-natured smile that was so 'Charlie.'

"Did someone say something to you about Clyde?" His question was a little sharper than he probably intended, which raised my suspicions more. "Well, Remley would probably prefer I not mention this, but Clyde was her cousin. That's one reason she was so upset. She didn't want anyone to know, because it would seem that we only chose him to be our photographer because of the family link. He was really trying to get his business up and running."

That made sense. I knew it had to be something like that. Phew.

Chapter Twenty-six

Consider alternative activities for guests who don't wish to dance. A board game table is a good option. Set up a table or two designated for games, etc. in a quiet corner of your venue space. By providing an activity other than dancing, you will encourage guests to stay longer. It's a celebration for everyone, try to be inclusive.

On some level, I recognized that my relationship with Brian couldn't be a good one if I was scared to confide in him the true reason we were going to Sylvie's wedding…and the fact that we weren't invited. Fact is, I plain wanted to go and needed an escort. No, I needed to go, as I knew that I'd find something to help Addalee. And, as Brian was the detective heading the investigation that was trying to prove Addalee guilty, no, I didn't think he would be jumping with joy to help me. But wouldn't he want to find the truth? A little voice asked me. Well, I would certainly hope so. But sometimes when he thought something was a given, and he just had to prove it, he couldn't see any other way. And aren't we all that way, just a little? I guess that was my way of trying to excuse him, because frankly, I was disappointed in Brian. He *knew* Addalee. But Brian's words: "Most people are not bad people. I don't think Addalee is a bad person. That doesn't mean she couldn't have done a bad thing." Sigh.

The candlelight wedding and reception was black tie. He sure does clean up well, I thought of my handsome beau, as I studied Brian when he came to pick me up. I was walking down the stairs, making the grand entrance Ellis demanded. She and I had had such fun getting ready for tonight. She had done my hair, nails, and makeup—far better than I would have done them. I actually thought I might buy some of the cosmetics she used on me. I think she was practicing for her prom with Kevin in the spring. We had already started dress shopping. And boy was I lucky not to have a wedding today. I did have one booked, but the bride and groom had decided last-minute to elope to Las Vegas. Can you say perfect timing?

Brian still hadn't seen me; he was looking at his phone. Work or football score, I wondered. I was wearing a new gown, a deep green velvet 'A' line dress with a little drape at the waist, so good for us ladies of a certain age. My hair was in a low French twist with wispy tendrils framing my face. My mirror said my makeup was just right, and that was confirmed when Brian put his phone away and saw me. Yes, he actually did a double-take.

"Katie,' he whispered. You look; you look...perfect."

Well, if that isn't high praise, I don't know what is. I smiled my Katie smile.

"Thanks, Bri." I made it down the stairs without falling, thanks be to God. I was nervous with the heels I was wearing. I almost never wore such high heels, and they were new on top of the height risk. Brian helped me into my trusty navy wool winter dress coat; I grabbed my evening bag with all the essentials (if anyone needed a 'bride bag' tonight, they were out of luck) and kissed Ellis.

"Wait, wait," she said, moving us over to the center of the foyer. "I have to get a pic. You guys look too good." I slipped out of my coat and threw it on the stair banister, and Ellis snapped away. We did our duty and smiled. I had such a hard time looking natural in photos. I hoped this one came out well.

We climbed into Brian's Bronco; he held the door for me, of course, and we were off.

"So, tell me a little about who these people are, so I don't look like an idiot," Brian asked.

What to say, what to say?

"Well," I needed to make this good. "The bride is the kindergarten teacher Ellis is helping out for her community service hours." I held my breath.

"Well, that's kinda weird that you were invited, with a plus one no less." Brian had been around me long enough now to know that the plus one was a big deal. As numbers can be limited at weddings, and weddings as a whole are so expensive these days, it wasn't always given that a single guest could bring an additional guest. It had to be specifically stated on the invitation.

"Well, even though it's black tie, the bride and groom are just having a cocktail reception, so it's less expensive, so more people could come." And that way, hopefully, we wouldn't be caught crashing the wedding. As there would be no assigned seats, it was a good possibility I could pull it off. We weren't attending the church ceremony that had been earlier in the day—here would be more scrutiny there.

"Well, why isn't Ellis coming? That seems a more natural invite," Brian just wasn't letting it go.

"Brian, really, this is a cocktail party." I put just a tinge of scolding into my reply.

"Oh, yeah," he responded, duly chastened.

The reception was being held at the Wadsworth Mansion, a very popular reception site.

According to Wikipedia:

From its formal classical nucleus to the naturalized wilderness of its forest, literally every square foot of the estate was shaped by the ideas of Colonel Clarence S. Wadsworth and his architects. After marrying Katharine Fearing Hubbard, Col. Wadsworth began amassing land in the western part of Middletown that would eventually become his 600-acre (2.4 km²) estate. Starting in 1900, thousands of trees and shrubs were planted to change pastures and orchards into a naturalistic woodland setting around the mansion. Dense nursery plantations were established, and mature specimen trees were planted. Some pasturage was left in its natural state and open areas were set aside for a lawn tennis court, the great lawn south of the mansion, and formal gardens. John Charles Olmsted played a major role in the design of the estate. The full extent of Olmsted's influence on the final design is not really known, but the firm's well-known approach to landscape is evident.

The mansion's architect was Francis Hoppin, who was classically trained at Brown University, M.I.T., and the Ecole des Beaux-Arts in Paris. He became known for his country estates, most notably The Mount, Edith Wharton's 1902 home in Lenox, Massachusetts. The contract for the house was let to the Dennis O'Brien Construction company, a Middletown firm, at a cost of $90,000.00, a considerable sum even then. The use of reinforced structural concrete and fireproofing, considered a relatively new technology at the time, had rarely been used in residential buildings. Construction of the house began in 1908 and was 'completed' around 1911.

In 1994, the City of Middletown purchased the estate and the remaining 103 acres (0.4 km²) for $1,000,000.00. Over the next two years, the city evaluated and developed plans to restore the building and grounds. On June 25, 1996, the residents of Middletown approved a referendum for bond funding to rehabilitate the buildings and landscape. The project architect was David Scott Parker of Southport, Connecticut. The construction contractor was Kronenberger and Sons Restoration, a Middletown company specializing in the restoration of old structures. Due to unforeseen work, the costs of the rehabilitation were greater than budgeted, and the citizens approved additional bond funding in 1999. On December 30, 1999, the building received a Certificate of Occupancy just in time to open for a millennium wedding celebration. Over $5.6 million had been expended to restore the mansion.

I've done several weddings at the Wadsworth Mansion, and the physical building and staff never disappoint. Sometimes, the only issue with an event is the bad behavior of the family or guest.

The Wadsworth, like most venues, has a strict 'no alcohol before Cocktail Hour' policy. One time, at one of my weddings, the father of the groom wanted to bring a twelve-pack of beer into the venue to 'pre-game' during the photo session. He had flown up from down south on his private jet, and felt if he was renting the venue, it was his to do as he wished. (The bride's family was actually taking care of the bill for the venue).

The building supervisor politely told him the rules, and he immediately and rudely asked to speak to her superior. She said she was the person on duty that day, that there was no one to call. He began arguing and bullying her. She was close to tears. I finally stepped in and said that I was the building supervisor's boss today, and the final decision was to take his beer out and drink it in the parking lot if he had to. We stared at each other, but finally he blinked and went outside. Our encounters the rest of the day and evening were tense, however. I had made an enemy. Was it worth it? No, but then again, I hate to see someone bullied…so yeah, I guess it was.

I shrugged off those negative thoughts as Brian and I walked up the grand drive to the massive front door. The grounds were manicured to within an inch of their lives. They were pristine and lush. It didn't matter as much here at the Wadsworth if the bride had rain on her wedding day. Photos could still be taken outside on the grounds. All the ancient trees made a natural umbrella.

The front door was open, and I could hear music floating outside. We were still experiencing temperate weather before the harshness of winter, and the fall air felt feather-light on my skin. Even if tonight was a bust on the information-gathering front, I planned to have a good time. As long as Brian didn't realize we were real-life wedding crashers, *and* the bride didn't catch sight of me. She didn't really know me, but she knew me well enough to be aware that I shouldn't be there. I thought I could pull it off. I knew a wedding schedule pretty well, knew what parts, when, and where to avoid.

We entered and were immediately offered a glass of champagne by a male server dressed in tails and white gloves, no less. I smiled my thanks and took a glass. Brian did the same. We smiled at each other; Brian did that funny thing, making his eyebrows go up and down rapidly. I had to laugh.

As we entered the main ballroom, we were immersed in the crush of the guests and the servers carrying trays of appetizers. I made it a habit to never eat the Cocktail Hour food. Yes, it looks and smells divine, but there was just something about how it was waved through so many people. I think Covid has scared me for life. Always a germaphobe, I was manic about cleanliness now. I had eaten an orange and some almonds before Brian picked me up. I had told him to 'pre-game' the food, but he said he was fine eating the wedding fare. To each his own.

I didn't see anyone I knew, good. But I did hope to see someone I recognized to eavesdrop on.

As Sylvie Bunker was the bride, I was hoping to gather some intel on Clyde. He was her brother after all. I was a little surprised that the wedding went ahead after his death, but I also knew how devastatingly expensive it would be to reschedule. If a couple was okay going forward, I would encourage them to hold the wedding as planned.

Brian was making a meal of all the passed cocktail food and had found someone he knew and was chatting, in between chewing. I was a little worried about this. I hoped his friend didn't inquire too closely as to why we were in attendance. I couldn't worry about that now.

It was too early for the bride and groom to make their appearance, so I had a little time to operate in the open. When Sylvie and her groom made their grand entrance, I'd have to be more stealthy to avoid being spotted.

I looked down at my champagne glass, it was empty! I'd have to watch myself. I had to be as sober as possible to avoid being spotted, but as I never drink when I'm in charge of a wedding, it was a rare treat to do so tonight. I grabbed a glass from a passing waiter. I promised myself that I would take care with this glass and use as a prop.

I glanced back at Brian, and he was still with the gentleman he had struck up a conversation with. Now they were both looking at his phone, football scores for sure.

Good! That's a safe topic. I continued my wanderings, going just slowly enough to maybe catch a phrase or comment that would be helpful.

The wedding party was beginning to filter in, I noticed, as several ladies wearing the same dress appeared as if by magic. More often than not, brides allowed their bridesmaids to wear dresses that they themselves chose, as long as it was in a particular color palette. But their arrival told me I didn't have much time, not if I wanted to avoid the bride. So far, I had nothing. I wasn't sure what I thought I'd find or hear, but I had hopes. When I was about ready to drain my champagne glass and go find Brian to plead a headache and the need to go home, a passing bridesmaid said, "I feel so bad for Sylvie. She misses Clyde so much," a blond bridesmaid said softly to her friend.

"I know. I'm so glad that they went ahead with the wedding. I wasn't sure they would. Sylvie was ready to take the loss on the vendor retainers and deposits and just go to Vegas and elope." Said a redheaded bridesmaid.

"I'm so glad they didn't cancel. Clyde was so selfish, he never thought of anyone but himself. It would have made me see red if he had cheated sweet Sylvie out of this day."

The redhead bridesmaid gasped. "That's a little harsh, Brenda, don't you think?"

"No," Brenda replied, "I don't. Do you know what he had put Sylvie and her family through?" I took a big gulp of my champagne for something to do. I tried to appear engaged; the fact that it was with my champagne glass was not to be too closely scrutinized.

"You know he's in deep with Mr. Di'Rissi," said Brenda in a hushed tone. I had to lean in a little to hear them. Luckily, they had been hitting the champagne, I'd wager, and neither noticed.

"You're kidding me! I knew he was dating Maria, but didn't know it went further than that," said the other in horror. "Sylvie never said a *word* to me, and you know how close we are!" The raised eyebrows that Brenda offered her friend/friendship rival said otherwise.

"Like was he doing something *illegal*?" The horror was real in her voice. Brenda merely shrugged.

"I mean, he was involved, so what would you expect. And now…he's dead." Brenda declared the obvious in a dramatic fashion.

Laaaaadies and Gentlemen!" Boomed the DJ. "In just a moment, it will be my pleasure to introduce you to the brand-new Mr. and Mrs.!" It was his job to get the crowd pumped up. "What I need from you all is to form a circle around the ballroom floor with an opening by the grand staircase. Our bride and groom will be descending the staircase momentarily." Uh oh, time for me to go.

I looked around. I won't say frantically, but I *was* rather frantic to find Brian. I had overstayed my welcome. The last thing I needed was to come face to face with Sylvie. But I didn't see Brian anywhere. Brian, where are you? I screamed inside my head. I scanned the ballroom, nothing. Then I saw him. He was, of course, by the cheese station. He must be hungry, because he was shoveling food in his mouth as fast as he could. I had to smile. He was such a little boy at times.

I made my way over to him; it wasn't easy, however. "Hey, you," I put my hand on his forearm. He looked up and tried to smile around the food in his mouth.

"Bri, my stomach isn't good. I think we are going to have to go." Did I feel guilty lying? I did. I'm not sure what was worse: my lying about coming here, telling him we were invited, or lying about going home and saying I was sick. But actually, my stomach was upset…lies will do that to you.

Brian put a comforting hand on my back, and I almost told him the truth. His look of worry and caring was real. My words were not.

I already had my pocketbook, and we had checked no coats. My card had been put in the card/gift box, unsigned, of course, but with a generous cash gift. It was the least I could do. He guided me expertly out of the ballroom. We were definitely going against the flow of the guests attempting to make a circle for the bride and groom's intro.

When we finally hit the outside, I took a welcome breath of cool fall air and couldn't help it, I smiled. But too late, Brian saw it.

He stopped and turned toward me. "Katie, wait, you're faking, aren't you?" He was really and truly mad, and I don't blame him.

I wouldn't outright lie to him. My silence was my answer. Although if I were being honest, I had lied to him about the whole wedding.

"Urrrggggg," Brian yelled as he hot-footed it to his SUV. He didn't open my car door this time. I can't say I blamed him. I hobbled along in my too-high heels and got myself up into the elevated cab. This was not going to be a pleasant ride home. I looked at Brian out of the corner of my eye. His face was scarlet. I can only imagine the self-control it took for him not to scream at me. Progress on the temper front?

He drove out of the parking lot a little too fast, scattering gravel that had made its way to the lot from the walkways. I knew I was wrong, but I was right too. Brian and his force weren't looking at anyone except Addalee. I knew she wasn't the one who killed Clyde. I had to help her; no one else would, well, except Sarah.

Brian said not one word to me on the way back to my house. Not one word. He pulled into my driveway with too much speed and a rather reckless disregard to any pedestrians may be walking down the sidewalk. He was mad and justified, but his behavior wasn't okay. Just 'cause you're mad didn't give you a pass to be a jerk. Was I rationalizing a wee bit? Yeah, I was.

He was silent in the idling car. I waited, hoping he would say *something*. When he didn't, I reluctantly got out of the car and hopped down. I didn't look back as I made my way to my mudroom door. Brian did *not* wait until he saw that I got safely inside. If he didn't walk me to the door, he always made sure I was safely in the house until he drove off. This went back all the way to high school, at my mom's insistence. I felt my heart sink a little. Now I was mad too.

Chapter Twenty-seven

Will your dog be part of the wedding party or at least in the pre-ceremony photos? Including a pet is a very common occurrence among couples today. If you choose to do this, it's a good idea to make arrangements for the dog to be cared for post-ceremony. A wedding reception is not the place for a pet. You want to enjoy your day, not worry about your dog. The potential for injury is great as well, from cars, or just too much shared food. What to do? Hire a pet sitter, or a company to come and pick the dog up, and keep them until you can retrieve your pet. Or better yet, just include your dog in your engagement photo shoot and not the wedding itself.

I woke the next morning with a heavy heart. I hoped Brian could call or text last night, but he didn't. I sent an 'I love you' text, as well as an 'I'm sorry' text, to no response. All this, and I really hadn't found out anything important. I already knew that Clyde was involved with the Di'Rissi family, but not that he was doing illegal things; well, I guess I still didn't know for sure.

I just couldn't leave it alone with Brian, although I knew that I should. So, I sent:

Brian—I know you're mad, and I can't say I blame you. But I know Addalee didn't kill Clyde, and I'm going to prove it—any way I can or have to. You won't consider any other suspects, so I don't know what else to do. I'm sorry I wasn't honest, but...I didn't know what else to say at this point).

I saw the bubbles working on the text app, but nothing came through right away. Then...

Katie, it's the same old story with you. You say you're sorry, but the lies keep coming. It's like you think you're excused from them if you say, 'sorry.' As if whatever you believe and are working toward is more important than everyone else's feelings. This isn't working for me. I've got some late nights ahead; I won't be by for a while.

I felt my stomach drop. Then I felt sick. I knew there was truth to his words. What I had to decide was how committed I was to Addalee. Was I willing to sacrifice my relationship for her?

Well, not for her per se, but for the truth. I had to. I decided not to even respond to Brian. What could I say?

I picked up my phone and opened the text app again.

What are you doing right now? I asked Sarah.

Just finished writing an offer on a two-million-dollar home. What are YOU doing now?

Wow. She was killing it in the real estate market. *You free?*

Wide open until the owner responds. They have twenty-four hours to get back to me. When they do, then it's all hands on deck. What's up?

I'm doing a deep dive into the Ring doorbells on Addalee's street. Hope to provide her some sort of alibi with the time stamps if she appears on any, or her car does.

I'm in—Jen's in ten?

Yup

Sarah beat me to Jen's and was already seated at our table. Today she was dressed in 'Sarah Casual.' This consisted of straight leg jeans that had just been washed enough for the perfect light blue color, Rothy flats in a deep cranberry, a matching belt, and a cream cashmere cardigan sweater. She even had a cranberry-colored headband to match. Double pearl earrings bounced against her neck gently when she looked up at my entrance.

I was dressed in jeans too, although somehow, I don't think I looked as chic. I didn't have a belt, and my shoes were plain old white lace-up Keds. Today I had a blue and white striped button-down shirt, which had been washed and dried to just the perfect softness. I threw a corduroy L.L. Bean jacket over for a little warmth. I loved the ensemble, so there was that. I may not look as put together as Sarah, but I was comfortable.

Sarah had already ordered our coffees, and they were on the table at our respective seats. I scanned the coffee bar for Jen. She must be out today; I'd have to catch up with her later. I missed her.

"Thanks for the coffee, Sarah," she really could be thoughtful…at times. "Smart to get them 'to go.' Are you ready to do this? I was thinking maybe we could incorporate a real estate canvas of the area for cover."

Sarah looked displeased. "Ah, no. I'm not pulling my business into this harebrained scheme of yours."

How rude! "Harebrained? I thought you were on board with helping Addalee!"

"Re-lax, Manet, I'm just yanking your chain. I'm on board, but I am serious about keeping my business out of it.

"Understood. Let's roll." We both stood up. "I guess the best thing to do is to go to her neighborhood and just start knocking on doors."

Addalee and her husband, Cory, lived on Main Street, but about a half mile from here. Sarah and I decided without speaking that we could walk. It was another beautiful fall day. The day was golden, with the gentle wind blowing a few orange, red, and yellow leaves tumbling down the street.

We arrived in front of Addalee and Cory's house. "I think it might be a good idea to ask Cory and Addalee if they want to join us. I can't imagine they'd mind, but maybe we should ask." I said.

We climbed the porch steps of Cory and Addalee's home and knocked on the door. The house looked like no one was home, and no one answered.

"Well, heck. I say we just go and ask questions, anyway, see if anyone has footage of the day and time. What could it hurt?" Sarah reasoned.

"I agree." We started down the street and saw Mrs. Rogers, our high school English teacher, rocking on her front porch.

"Well, I'll be. If it's not Sarah Deloro and Katie Manet," said Mrs. Rogers with a cackle. "I would have recognized her anywhere. Her face was the same smooth skin, but her beautiful black hair was now white as snow, and she was thinner, rather frail. "I never thought I'd see the two of you together. Weren't you enemies in high school?" She frowned.

"We've grown up a little since then, Mrs. Rogers," I said.

"Oh, Katie, you always were the innocent one. You two will never *really* be friends. Who ended up with Brian McAllister?"

Sarah directed a thumb at me. "This one," but she smiled.

"Come on up to the porch and sit awhile," Mrs. Rogers invited.

"That's so nice of you, Mrs. Rogers, but we…" I started.

"That would be great, Mrs. R." Sarah interrupted me. I stole a glance at Sarah, but didn't say anything.

We both climbed up the porch steps and sat in the cushy chairs Mrs. Rogers indicated.

"Celia," Mrs. Rogers screeched. "My daughter-in-law's here cleaning. At least she's good for something," she said with no humor.

"Wow!" I mouthed to an equally startled Sarah as Mrs. Rogers turned her head to yell again at her daughter-in-law.

"Celia! We have company! Fetch some tea and cookies!" She ordered. Apparently, Mrs. Rogers hadn't changed much. She was always ordering students around in her classroom, too.

A pretty, but harried, young woman came to the old-fashioned screen door, one with the screen on top and wood on the bottom. "Coming right up, Miss Betty." Then she noticed us.

"Oh! Hello!"

"Hi," I spoke first, and introduced Sarah and myself.

"Nice to meet you," she said politely, if a little quietly. "I'll be right out with the tea."

"And don't forget the cookies!" Bellowed Mrs. Rogers.

"I told Ben not to marry that girl!" Mrs. Rogers told us, and not quietly either. Was she losing it?

Sarah spoke up this time. "She seems like a lovely woman, and how nice of her to help you with the house.

"Humph," was all Mrs. Rogers replied.

"So why are you girls really here?" She turned her eagle's eye first to Sarah and then to me.

Sarah opened her hand and turned to me in a 'all you' gesture.

"Well, you remember Addalee Baker, right, Mrs. Rogers?"

"Of course I do, what a dear girl, and beautiful too. She was always a favorite of mine." She smiled fondly.

"Well, she's in a bit of a fix. Did you hear about that photographer that was murdered?' Sarah jumped in.

"I did read about it in the "Eastbury Citizen," (our local weekly gossip sheet), "nasty thing. What is our world coming to?" She shook her head in despair. "Wait, you're not suggesting that Addalee has been accused of this heinous crime? Impossible!" She crossed her soft arms across her chest in a huff.

"That is *exactly* what is happening, Mrs. Rogers!" I said with feeling.

"So why are you here? How can I help?" She sat up a little straighter.

"We're trying to help Addalee get some sort of alibi by checking out neighbors' ring cameras. Maybe one caught her with a timestamp on it to prove she couldn't have killed Clyde—the photographer. His body was found all the way across town. It could be anything from her car going by your house, or Addalee walking her dog. She said she was out that night, just getting some air, walking her dog, etc. But no one could prove that."

"Well, that is a dandy idea, Katie, did you come up with that all by yourself?' Did Mrs. Rogers seem a little condescending? "But I'm sorry, I don't have one of those doorbell camera things. Ben wants me to get one, but I think they're just a waste of money." Ben was Mrs. Rogers's son.

Celia chose that moment to come through the screen door carrying a tray of iced tea and a plate of what looked to be homemade chocolate chip cookies. The items on the tray rattled slightly, either because it was heavy, or she was nervous. My money was on nerves.

"Celia!" Mrs. Rogers bellowed. "Iced tea? It's October! Surely you know we drink hot tea in October!" Mrs. Rogers's face flushed in her ire. The items on the tray rattled even more.

"Sorry, Miss Betty." Celia turned to go back into the kitchen when Mrs. Rogers stopped her.

"Oh, my stars, just put it *down,* Celia, for God's sake." Celia set the tray down and turned to go.

I reached out to gently touch Celia's arm. "Join us, please, Celia. It would be nice to visit with you, and maybe you saw something."

"About Addalee?" she said softly. "She's just a lovely lady. I'd love to help in any way if I can. I couldn't help overhearing." She blushed.

"We are trying to figure out if anyone saw Addalee in the neighborhood the night Clyde was killed. It was the night of October 2. Were you here, or were you at home?"

"Was that a Tuesday?" Celia asked.

"Yes," Sarah answered.

"I thought so. You know I give the nurse the night off on Tuesdays, Miss Betty. I stay the night in the guest room," Celia explained as she looked at Sarah and me. "Miss Betty requires twenty-four-hour care, so we do what we can."

"Very generous of you," Sarah said to Celia, giving Mrs. Rogers a look. She didn't realize how lucky she was. She most certainly should treat her lovely daughter-in-law better. Mrs. Rogers was outright mean, but then she hadn't been the sweetest teacher in high school.

Celia looked up at the covered porch, painted blue like the sky as tradition dictated, trying to remember.

"So, I had been watching the television show "Will Trent" that night on a recording. Miss Betty had taken her evening meds, and I was turning off the TV and downstairs lights. This was about 10:00. I started walking up the stairs when I heard two dogs fighting. I went to the door, and there was Addalee with her two dogs. They were both on their hind legs, at each other's throats. Addalee was really upset. She finally got her water bottle out of her pocketbook, a big old thing, and threw it on them. She walked by the house several times for a couple of hours. I was close to asking her in, but," and here she looked at Mrs. Rogers, "I wasn't sure Miss Betty would like it. I never really thought about it the next day."

Sarah and I jumped up and grabbed Celia. First Sarah and then me. I hugged her a little too tightly, based on the grunt she expelled.

"Celia, this is just what we hoped! You can put Addalee in a time and spot that she couldn't have killed Clyde. Your house is too far from where Clyde was killed." Why wasn't she questioned before? Probably because she didn't live here, and if the cops did a door-to-door canvas, she may not have been visiting Mrs. Rogers. But that was just a guess.

Then Celia confided that her husband, Mrs. Roger's son, Ben, had installed a doorbell camera anyway, even though Mrs. Rogers wasn't in favor of it. I felt a little thrill. We asked to see Celia's Doorbell Videos to make sure Addie was in the neighborhood the entire time when Clyde would have been killed. It showed Addie in several clips. There would have been no time for her to get to Clyde's neighborhood and back, plus don't forget…killing him with her bow and arrow.

"I really helped," Celia sounded shocked and rather hesitant. I saw her eyes slide to her mother-in-law. But thank goodness Mrs. Rogers smiled benignly at her.

I fired off a text to Addalee, and Celia let me share the Doorbell videos with her. I advised her to email them to Brian ASAP. Addalee responded right away with ten red hearts.

Chapter Twenty-eight

If you choose a wedding cake that has buttercream frosting, make sure it can be refrigerated until right before the guests arrive. You don't want your cake to melt! Better yet, consider fondant for your cake. It won't melt if you don't have access to a fridge and stands up to humidity as well as heat. It photographs beautifully.

I was doing one of my groom's a *big* favor. He had forgotten to pick up his bride's wedding band at Eastbury Jewelers. He called me in a panic and all but begged me to pick it up for him. They were going to have the rings blessed this weekend at his church, and his control freak bride-to-be would indeed freak out if he didn't have her ring. He really didn't have to beg; I've done far worse, ha ha. Besides, I loved visiting with Mr. Parker at Eastbury Jewelers.

I opened the shop's door and was greeted to first a merry jingle of sleigh bells attached to the door and next….to an empty shop. I could hear a low rumbling of voices, however. Mr. Parker must be in the back with someone. I made myself at home, drooling over the gorgeous jewelry. Grant, my ex, had never been a big gift-giver, until the last year of our marriage, when I got some 'guilt' gifts for his flagrant cheating with our next-door neighbor. I thought about selling the over-the-top gifts, but jewelry is jewelry, I thought. I touched the two-carat solitaire I had hanging around my neck that used to be my engagement ring.

Mr. Parker walked out of the back room, saw me, and his face blanched. He was as white as a marshmallow. He frantically shook his head at me, mouthing "No!"

I looked to the left, to the right, hopping around like a scared rabbit. Why exactly was I so frantic? Well, I guess because Mr. Parker was. I finally hopped behind a three-panel screen, which Mr. Parker used to give his couples some privacy as they filled out the paperwork on any financing involved with an engagement ring purchase.

The color was returning to Mr. Parker's face. He looked over his shoulder and was apologizing to someone, but glancing my way, well, toward the screen I was hiding behind. He made a shushing motion with his mouth while continuing to try to pacify the person behind him. I'd have to pay attention. I wanted to know who Mr. Parker was talking to. I snuck another peek between two of the panels and saw...Brian! walk from the back office following Mr. Parker, and he was agitated.

"Mr. Parker!" Brian's voice was low, but I knew him well enough to know he was angry and trying to control it. "I do not understand how you could lose it?"

"I didn't lose it, Brian," Mr. Parker was the one on the verge of anger now. "I don't lose my inventory."

"Well, it really isn't your inventory, is it, Mr. Parker?" At this exchange, Brian's voice was a little harsher. "It's my damn ring, well, my grandmother's, and I trusted you with it!"

Oh...my...God! It was Brian, and he could only be referring to one ring, the ring I thought for sure he'd propose to me with. And it appears that was his plan. I felt a lump forming in my stomach, almost a lump of dread. Was it because the ring was misplaced, or was it something else? Was it the fact that I wasn't ready? Would I ever be? Was Brian trying to reclaim the ring because he had changed his mind? I saw Mr. Parker glance my way. I stepped back from the screen. I did *not* want to be seen.

"Brian," now Mr. Parker sounded apologetic. "I have no idea what could have happened. It was filed under your name in the repair folder and now..."

"Well, did you look under Kate's name?" Brian sounded exasperated. Brian moved to the customer side of the counter. I was happy to see that he wasn't going to physically put pressure on poor old Mr. Parker. Brian had to know that this was an accident. He had been our town's trusted jeweler for forty-plus years.

Mr. Parker sighed heavily and raked his hand through his gray, thinning hair. "I just don't know, Brian. I looked for the ring under your name, Kate's maiden name, her married name." Here, Mr. Parker looked right at me. How did Brian not know I was there? But thank God he didn't. That would just make this whole thing even worse.

"I'll be back tomorrow at this time, Mr. Parker," Brian spoke in a low tone, but I knew how angry he was. "And I'll expect to have my ring sitting on that little velvet cushion," he indicated a lush pillow behind the counter on the work counter. He left in a huff, giving the sleigh bells on the door a nasty little shake as he closed the door a little too hard.

I crept around from behind the screen. I felt badly for Mr. Parker. He had to feel terrible as well as embarrassed.

"Katie, I don't know what to say. I'm so sorry to ruin the surprise, and I'm sick about the status of the ring." He looked as sick as a dog who pulled a pound of bacon off the kitchen counter and indulged.

I put my hand on his across the glass-topped counter. "I'm sure it will turn up, Mr. Parker. And then you'll say to yourself, Oh! I remember now!" I smiled to soften my words even more.

Mr. Parker still looked crestfallen. "I feel sick at ruining the surprise." He said again and looked so sad. As he worked in the world of engagements, Valentine's Day, anniversaries, and other special events, this was a man who believed in love and happy times. He sure didn't look happy now.

"It really wasn't a surprise, Mr. Parker. I had an inkling. And besides, I'm not big on surprises; I like to know what's going on." Not true, but I wanted him to feel better. I actually loved surprises. There's nothing I like more than a good surprise party. But in reality, I did know this was coming. I just had to decide how I felt about it. It scared me a little that I wasn't particularly excited. I left a despondent Mr. Parker frantically looking for Brian's ring. I hoped he'd find it soon, for his sake. But in all actuality, I wouldn't mind if it took a little while to find…it would give me more time to think.

Chapter Twenty-nine

Wedding favors: Do you want to give your guests wedding favors? If you do, make sure it is something consumable. No one wants a trinket that has your name and wedding date on it. Some ideas: candy, honey, vinegar, or even scratch lottery tickets. Simply put, something to eat or one-use items are the most 'favor'-able.

While I was thrilled that Sarah and I had found someone to support Addalee's alibi, it made me feel less guilty about my caper with Brian. Okay, my lying escapade. I'd call it by name. Why couldn't he do that? Why did he have to focus on her, and instead of trying to prove her innocent, only focus on her possible guilt? I knew that Cory's mom, Addalee's mother-in-law, had never liked Addie and would be ready to get her out of their lives. And yes, she had an 'in' with the Eastbury chief of police. But they weren't corrupt. I knew Brian wasn't, but I was disappointed.

I guess my mission was complete. Addalee had an alibi. I had gotten involved in this case because of her, but now, my curiosity was piqued. Where would Brian go from here?

Apparently, the thought of him conjured up the incoming text.

Addalee and Cory were just here with Celia Rogers. Celia gave Addalee the alibi she needed. You were right, Katie. But I don't like your lying.

Wow! I was so proud of Addalee for going the extra mile and taking Celia, the video, and Cory straight to the police station. And…was Brian really apologizing? Well, if he could apologize, I could also let some things go. I would just have to accept that I wasn't the professional crime solver and Brian was. He had to have a reason to run the case as he was now.

I sorry for lying, Brian. Want to have dinner tonight? We can go to Luigi's. My treat.

I inserted a heart emoji. Luigi's was a place we saved for celebrations. I thought it appropriate.

I saw the texting bubbles, but no words came. Then…

I'd love that, Katie. My heart soared.

* * *

I left a chicken Caesar salad in the fridge for Ellis. She had a late practice and would get a ride home with a teammate. I had had quite a time getting ready for my dinner with Brian tonight. I wanted to send the right message, only problem, I didn't know what that message was. I finally decided on a black cashmere long-sleeved belted dress. It was understated, but luxurious. I had the sweetest, thin as tissue, pink cashmere shawl to pair it with. I wore heels that were much higher than usual, and my best pearls—a 'tin cup necklace' (you know the necklace that Renee Russo wore in every scene of the movie "Tin Cup" with Kevin Costner). I was obsessed with that necklace. It had a fine gold chain spaced every inch with an 8 mm creamy pearl. My earrings were pearls as well, a two-pearl per earring number that dangled saucily against my neck. I even wore a little more makeup than my usual—wearing eye pencil to accentuate my eyes. My eyes, in my mind, were my best feature.

The doorbell rang, and I had to answer it myself, no Ellis, tonight, so I could make a grand entrance. I opened the door to a ruddy-cheeked Brian. It looked like he had spent the day in the wind and sun; he probably had. He was freshly shaven, my favorite, unless he had several days of scruff; that was appealing too. He handed me a posy of violets, my number one flower. I have no idea where he could have rounded them up. They were usually in season in June. It was such a simple bouquet, but it spoke to my heart. It hit me, all of a sudden. No one was perfect; I surely wasn't. Why did I expect Brian to be? Was it because Grant had been so imperfect. I was looking for the perfect man? I'd never find him, I realized. I would just be glad that I had someone who cared for me, who could say 'I'm sorry,' who tried to be a better person. That was my Brian. I smiled, took a step toward him, and he grabbed me and picked me up right off my feet. The kiss he gave me wasn't chaste or friendly, or just a 'hello.' It was filled with all the pent-up passion he had for me. He finally put me down, and we just looked at each other and grinned.

"Let's go to dinner," I said. I didn't even let him in the door, we might not make it to dinner if I did, so, I grabbed my delicious pink cobweb of a wrap and we went out to Brian's SUV.

We were quiet as we drove to Luigi's, but I leaned into Brian, and we held hands. It seemed like such a teen thing to do, but it felt right. After we parked in the restaurant lot, Brian kissed me again, promising more later.

I had been on pins and needles for weeks, expecting a proposal from Brian, and then feeling gutted that maybe we were done. So, when the waiter came with dessert and champagne, I just thought Brian was being festive.

He was quiet as the waiter opened the bottle and poured us each a glass. He added a little, "Enjoy."

Then Brian put his hand in his pocket and took my hand with his other.

"Katie, I've thought and rethought how to do this a million ways, but I decided to do it genuinely. Because that's what I want, a genuine union." He opened his hand, and there was the most exquisite ruby and diamond ring, his grandmother's ring. Mr. Parker must have found it. Okay, I'm shallow. I quickly did an assessment. The ruby center stone was at least three carats, and the round diamonds to the side were at least a carat each, all set in, I'd believe, eighteen-carat gold. Oh my gosh!

"Will you marry me?"

"Yes," I said softly, "but Brian...your temper." I paused. How would he react? But I had to say something. It had to be addressed.

Brian flushed. "Katie. I'm seeing someone to help me with anger management."

I opened my mouth to respond, but he cut me off.

"No, it isn't the department giving me an ultimatum. I just know it's the right thing to do. Even I see I'm getting out of hand." Then I grabbed his—his hand that is, and squeezed, hard.

"Let me say it again, with more enthusiasm." I grinned. "Yes, yes, yes! I'm so proud of you!' I knew that by saying yes, I was also saying yes to starting a family. That wasn't guaranteed, but Brian was agreeing to the unknown, too. I felt lucky and excited. I couldn't wait to tell my girls, Ellis, Jen, and yes, Sarah. I knew she might be the happiest for me. She knew what a good guy he was. Would she be a bridesmaid if we had a big 'do'? Well, we will see, but I wouldn't be surprised.

Chapter Thirty

This is for the wedding guests. When traveling to a wedding via bus, car, or a walk from your hotel room to the ceremony space, allow travel time plus a little extra time to great friends/family and time to find your seat. Remember, you job is to wait on the bride's entrance, not the other way around.

I wasn't so concerned with Brian's flares of temper any longer, he had calmed down since our engagement, and I'm sure the therapy was helping. But I was concerned with all the mishaps surrounding him from the lost suit to cancelled restaurant reservations, to the misplaced ring. I'm glad I had finally come to a decision about our relationship. I still hadn't wrapped my head around it. I was in a daze, a happy daze. It seemed…surreal. I had married Grant right out of college. I had just turned twenty-two and had Ellis ten months later—at twenty-two. I had gone from high school to college to marriage. I had never been on my own, and I have to say…I now loved it. How would adding being answerable to another person again throw into the mix? Home-life, chores, budgets, schedules, would all have to be factored in. I was almost thirty-nine, still young enough to have that baby Brian wanted, and if I was honest, I really wanted it too. I had been too scared to hope for another child. Grant and I had wanted more kids, but after a miscarriage when Ellis was two, it never happened. We later found out that Grant's sperm count was low. Brian and I would have to act soon, given my age. Addalee and I were the same age, and she had confided to me that her obstetrician classified her as a 'geriatric' mother.

Even though Brian and I were back on track with our relationship, I needed to figure out what was going on with the botched plans Brian had been trying to make for our engagement. I felt fairly confident that someone had been sabotaging him and his attempts to propose. I could think of one person. Grant. My ex had made no secret of the fact that he wasn't a fan of Brian. This was just the type of thing he would do. I was incensed. How did I not suspect him and his evil doings from the very first event? Because things happen. Cut yourself some slack, I said gently to myself. Well, I was going to call Grant out now on this nonsense.

I pulled my cell from my pocket and punched in his number. He answered on the first ring.

"Kate! How are you?"

The bastard. "Nice, Grant, real nice." I felt my anger bubbling like my mom's caramel sauce right before she turned the heat off the burner to let it cool.

"Usually, I know why you're mad, Kate, and I have time to get my story straight. But this time, I don't know. What's up?" The jerk sounded sincerely perplexed. Oh, he was good.

"Grant," I sighed. "I don't have time for this today." I heard the wariness in my own voice. For the first time since I went down this road, thinking Grant was the saboteur of my marriage proposal from Brian, I was having my doubts. *Could* it be someone else?

"For old time's sake, let's cut to the chase, Grant. Are you messing with Brian? Sabotaging plans Brian has made, made for him and me?"

Silence. "No, Kate. I do have a life. Brian isn't my favorite person, but I have better things to do that mess with your plans." I was embarrassed. I realized how self-absorbed it sounded.

It was my turn to be quiet. Then, "I'm so sorry, Grant. I listened to myself and realized what a pill I'm being. Apologies. But someone *is* messing with him, and it doesn't feel good."

Grant chuckled good-naturedly. "I was a very good bet, Kate. But not guilty this time. But ask yourself, if not me, who else loves you and not Brian?" I chose to ignore the 'loves you' part. And it hit me…my dad. Dad was never a fan of Brian's. He liked him and all, but even back in high school, Brian discussed law enforcement. He wasn't really the one my father would have picked for me. And didn't he 'forget' to tell me that long-ago night in high school that Jen had come to our house looking for me? I now know she wanted to tell me about a note from Brian, hoping we could reconcile after a serious break-up. That note would have probably gotten us back together. But would Dad have gone to those extremes at this time in my life? I was doing well in my career, was happy…Only one way to find out. I'd have to go see my dad.

I had almost forgotten Grant on the other end of the line until I heard, "Kate, you still there?" Oops.

"Still here." I hoped he hadn't realized I had forgotten he was on the line.

"Forgot I was still on the line, didn't you?" I expected laughter, but didn't get any. "Story of my life." He sounded sad.

"Sorry for the call, Grant. I was a jerk."

"Never be sorry to call, Katie." He called me Katie in only moments of great tenderness. It wasn't lost on me.

"I'll check in soon," I said softly. "We can maybe have a family dinner. We need to discuss Ellis's college financial aid packages." I thought I'd throw him a bone.

He was gracious. "Sounds good, Kate." And he clicked off.

* * *

I put my phone in my back pocket of my jeans and grabbed my pocketbook and keys to my Suburban. I was going to make an unannounced visit to my parents. Was my mom sharing her observation of Brian's tantrum at the dry cleaner a clue? Was she trying to tell me something? Only one way to find out.

I didn't speed, but I did drive with purpose for the one point five miles from my house to my parents. Neither car was in the driveway, but that wasn't surprising as they kept their cars in the garage.

I parked in the drive, slammed my suburban door, and beep-beeped her

151

locked. I hustled to the front door. I was mad now, convinced my father was behind the meddling in my life.

I didn't knock. That's how it was done. This was my home too, even though I lived a mile and a half away. I entered the foyer and took the wide hallway to the family room, where my dad was watching some sort of game. With all the channels we now had access to, there could always be a game found. My dad looked up and smiled. He looked so tenderly at me, one of his beloved girls. I had a younger sister as well as a brother, but I secretly always thought I was Dad's favorite. Maybe all kids thought this, I hope so.

"Katie!" my dad's grin widened. He had put on a few pounds since his retirement from the fire department, and I know it concerned my mother. He still had a full head of the most gorgeous hair, though. It used to be red but was now a snowy white. He stood, then walked over and embraced me in a bear hug as if he hadn't seen me in a year. I hugged him back. My hero as a child and my hero now. One man who was always there for me.

"Can I get you a cup of coffee?" He started walking to the kitchen. Ever since I had absconded with my mom's favorite percolator, my parents' new pride and joy was their De'Longhi espresso machine. I know his increase in caffeine had both his mom and his cardiologist uneasy.

"No thanks, Dad. Can we sit?"

"Sure, Katie," Dad said as he sat back down in his La-Z-Boy. I chose the sofa. Oh boy. Now, when I was here, I didn't know where to start. Well, out with it, I told myself.

"Dad, do you know anything about Brian wanting to propose?"

Dad's face turned red. Ah ha! I knew it!

"Katie," Dad looked so sad. I don't know how I could be mad at him. I was though.

"Dad," I replied, trying to give him the serious face he deserved. If he really was the one playing those mean tricks on Brian and me, it was not okay. He had to know I was not going to stand for it.

"How could you, Dad? Do you not think I am adult enough to make my own decisions?" My anger was real now.

"Will you give me a minute, Katie? I can explain." I crossed my arms over my chest and leaned against the sofa back. All I had to do was stick out my bottom lip, and I was back in grade school, angry at my dad because he had called my teacher about a B on a science project when he felt certain that I deserved an A.

"It's not that I have anything against Brian; I just don't think you're ready. You're about to jump from one relationship right into another, and that was a failed one, too." Ouch. That stung, but it was true.

"So let me get this straight. You cancelled our dinner reservations, did something with Brian's suit at the dry cleaners, and…wait, did you do something with Brian's grandmother's ring? How in the world could you pull that off?" Who was this man?

My dad looked chagrined. He should have looked embarrassed. Did my mom know about this? I bet she did.

"Did Mom know?"

"Your mother and I don't have many secrets, but she didn't know about this. Ah, Katie, I knew it was wrong. But you just seem so fragile, and I didn't know how to help. It's not that Brian can't be right for you; it's just that he isn't now. Maybe you're not right for him. I just thought things were going too quickly and wanted to put the brakes on things a little. If the few road bumps I put up didn't make a difference, then maybe you were good to go. If not, then…"

I didn't know what to say, and was afraid if I spoke too soon, I'd say something I'd regret. So, I tried to put myself in his shoes. Would I do the same if Ellis was involved in a situation such as mine—at my age? Be honest, I told myself. Yeah, I bet I would. That doesn't mean I wasn't furious with my father…but maybe, just maybe, he had a point.

So instead of scolding him, I asked him how he hid the ring at the jewelry store.

"I just went in to say hello to old Mr. Parker and waited until he went in the back to clean a lady's ring and went through his repair drawer. All of us long-time customers know where that is. And I filed it under Becky Welch."

"Who is Becky Welch?" asked.

"Heck if I know," and we both laughed.

"And the dry cleaner and Brian's suit, how did that go missing?"

"Oh, Katie," Dad said, shaking his head. "How many years did I get my uniforms cleaned there. One ask, and the suit was 'misfiled.'

I wasn't even going to question the cancelled dinner reservation. One phone call, and that was done. My dad. I decided to let it go. I really couldn't fault him if I'd do the same. We had that coffee. I'd never admit this to anyone, but Dad's espresso was better than my percolator.

Chapter Thirty-one

Thank you notes: Yes, you must send a handwritten thank you note to each guest who gives you a gift. If two people give you one gift together, you must send each a note, unless it's a married couple. No, you can't text a thank you. No, you cannot email a thank you. Some things don't change. This is one of those things. One cute idea I saw...the bride and groom sent handwritten thank yous, but they also followed up with a photo of them using/enjoying the wedding gift and texted it to their guests. It was a hit.

If Clyde's murderer wasn't Addalee, and we knew she wasn't, then who was? I was sitting in my home office scrolling through my socials on my phone, basically killing time because I didn't want to work. But the thought remained, who killed Clyde? I paused a moment to look at my gorgeous engagement ring. I was thankful that Mr. Parker had done an appraisal, and Brian had already opened an insurance policy on it. I wouldn't have worn it otherwise. And it fit perfectly!

I got out a pad of paper, I always thought better when I wrote. I made a list of suspects. The suspects weren't necessarily mine.

1. Addalee. We had debunked that one.
2. Maria, Clyde's ex-girlfriend. What is the old adage? It's always the partner, husband/wife, boyfriend, or girlfriend. Maria had a lot to be mad about. But there was no motive for her except anger. It would have had to be a crime of passion. And killing someone with a bow and arrow seemed very premeditated to me.

3. 'Unknow' I needed to follow up on what Sylvie had said about her suspicions that Clyde had already started seeing someone new, which contradicted the fact that Clyde seemed to be trying to win Maria back. Whoever she was, she would have a powerful motive if she knew that Clyde was trying to win Maria back, with a house on the Cape, no less.

4. Gene, Clyde's work associate with Mr. Di'Rissi or even Mr. Di'Rissi himself. This seemed very likely, as we already know they were involved in illegal activities, or we assume they are just by association.

5. The Doc—I crossed his name off. It felt good to check someone off.

6. Charlie made that list, but I can't believe it would be him. But on the list, he had to go.

I picked up my phone again and opened the text app. I'd figure out a plan with the help of my partner in crime, Sarah.

Are you free? I texted.

Nope. She texted back. I waited for more, but none came.

Can you text me when you are?

A thumbs-up came back.

What was I going to do with myself until Sarah texted me back? It could be hours. I opened my laptop and tried to get some work done on the seating chart for my next wedding. I was ready to pull my hair out. I couldn't make the numbers work with the qualifiers that the bride and groom had sent me. 'Aunt Mabel' can't sit with more than six people, but can't sit next to her ex-husband, but must sit with all her children; however, her ex wants to sit with the children too…I threw my hands up in frustration. I would have to have a sit-down with Floyd and Clara; I couldn't do this alone. I messaged them a calendar link requesting they choose a day and time so we could finish the seating chart.

I'm open now—what's up? Sarah texted.

Not sure where you are for the best meeting place? I asked.

In my office, come on by.

Be there in five. I responded.

I grabbed my phone, jumped into my white Keds (they paired nicely with my nude-colored tights and just above the knee jean skirt, with a white button-down long-sleeved shirt, of course). I headed off down Main Street to Sarah's office.

Sarah had a primo office on Main Street. It was decorated so warmly; you *wanted* to go in and beg her to sell your house or buy one of her listings. The flowerboxes out front, under her windows, were blooming with seasonal mums as always. They were bright yellow and made me happy.

I opened the door and was greeted by Elizabeth, Sarah's receptionist. Elizabeth had been an acquaintance in high school who had had a rough marriage. But Sarah stepped in and helped Elizabeth and gave her a job. When I found out how she had helped Elizabeth last spring, my opinion of Sarah changed. She was no longer the mean high school girl. She was actually a kind person underneath her hard shell. She'd never admit to it, though.

Elizabeth smiled, "Hey, Katie! How are you today?" She glowed with health and beauty. That wasn't always the case.

I smiled back. "I'm great, Elizabeth. Is Sarah available? We have an appointment."

"She sure is. Sarah told me to get your coffee order as soon as you come in and send you back to her office."

"I'll take a non-fat Cappuccino, thanks, Elizabeth," I said as I walked through the bright open concept to Sarah's glass-fronted office. She waved me in when she saw me. Sarah's office was much like her, sleek, all business, and expensive looking. Today she was dressed in a grey-blue cashmere sweater and a black pencil skirt, and of course, the required three-inch heels. I bet she was over six feet tall in that get-up.

I sat down on one of the guest chairs. "Coffee's on the way," she said. "What's up?"

"First, how's the doc holding up with his radiation treatment?" I asked about her beau, and Sarah's face softened.

"He's doing okay. No cancer treatment is ever easy on anyone. But he doesn't complain. Thanks for asking, Katie." Sarah's smile was genuine.

I'm glad he's doing as well as he is." I paused, then jumped in. "I want to pick your brain about Clyde's murder. Brian wants me to stay out of it, but…"

"Little Katie can't let it go," she said with a snark, that came back remarkably early after our earlier warm exchange.

Didn't make me feel very good. "Wow, way to play nice, Sarah." I was miffed with her.

Sarah, rather dramatically, threw her head down on her folded arms on her desk.

"Uuuugggg—sorry, Katie," I'm in the worst mood. I have the clients from hell. It has been a strain being nice and accommodating all morning." I had to laugh, and then she did too.

"So, you can't let it go. What are we going to do about it? What new adventures do you have planned for us?" Sarah said, but she smiled.

I scooted way down in my seat, stretching my back. "That's just it, I don't know who to focus on or what to do. I did make a list of suspects," I held the paper with the suspect's name aloft.

"Gimme," Sarah held out her hand and then snatched the paper. After reading it over, she said, "Well, we are going to have to figure out a way to talk to some of these people. And crashing a wedding is not the way to do it," she quirked an eyebrow at me.

"Heard about that, did you?"

"Everybody has heard about it," Yikes, I thought.

Chapter Thirty-two

If you are on a budget for your wedding, and very few people are not...think of what gives you the most bang for your buck. For example, if you're going to get a wedding cake anyway (FYI, not everyone has a wedding cake these days—some couples opt for pie, donuts, cupcakes, or a variety of desserts), buy a cake that's a little bigger than you need and make it a focal point, a décor item, if you will. Do you get a great value for your dollar for menus, or other printed items? In my opinion, no, but...it's not my opinion that matters, but yours.

We knew that Clyde was dating someone new, someone other than Maria Di'Rissi. That couldn't make Maria happy, a motive? Maybe the new woman had a motive, but we didn't know who she was. It shouldn't be that hard to figure out. I'd try Clyde's sister first, the newly married Sylvie. Sisters usually know what's going on in their brothers' lives, right? I had a younger brother, and while he was a general pain in the behind, I loved him. He was always the first in line to ask me for romantic advice when we were growing up. He was in a band now, traveling from gig to gig. In reality, I was waiting for him to grow up. He had a lovely girlfriend; of course, I knew all about her. See? I felt confident Sylvie would know about her brother's love life. My only worry, that Sylvie was on a honeymoon. My bet is that she and her new husband were waiting for summer break.

I would be picking Ellis up from her volunteer session at the elementary school and driving her to the high school today. It was raining, and I wasn't yet comfortable with her driving in inclement weather. A normal mom would wait out front. What excuse did I make to go into the classroom? Think, think. Why I'd buy a couple of children's books to add to the classroom library! Sometimes, I amazed myself. Now, next question, why wouldn't I just leave them in the school office to be delivered, or send them with Ellis? Hmm. Well, I was just that kind of person who had to present the gift myself so I could get thanks. I wonder if the staff would buy that? I'd give it a shot.

After stopping by the darling, well-stocked 'Riverbend Bookshop,' and picking out four children's best sellers, I headed over to the elementary school. I was buzzed in immediately and waved through to the kindergarten once I said I had a gift of books for Sylvie. The admin staff knew me now, and as I wasn't a threat, they weren't concerned about how I wanted to present my gift or not. I guess I thought a little too much of myself.

I waited just outside the kindergarten door while Ellis finished reading to the class. She had a sweet voice and a nice manner. Two little girls were sitting on either side of her, looking up at her adoringly.

"The end," she said dramatically, and slapped the book closed as I used to when I read to her as a child.

"Well, hello, Mrs. Ludlow," Sylvie said to me kindly. "Welcome!"

Ellis's head snapped up, and she looked at me. I couldn't tell if she was happy to see me…. or annoyed. Then she smiled. I guess I was in the all-clear.

"I come bearing gifts," I held the four books aloft, then took them to Sylvie. She squealed!

"Mrs. Ludlow! Wow, thank you! There is nothing we like better in Room Two than new books for our classroom library! What do you say, class?"

The sweet kindergarteners responded with an enthusiastic "Thank you!"

"We will read these after lunch if we can get all our seatwork done," Sylvie said with mock gravity. The little kindergarteners nodded their heads with extreme seriousness.

"Now, boys and girls, it's time to go to art. Mrs. Kington will be along in three minutes to collect you. If you're wearing pink, line up by the door." She continued calling colors until all the children were at the door and ready to go. A very tall blond woman, Mrs. Kington, I assume, came to get the children, and they walked off in two neat lines behind her.

"Thanks so much, Mrs. Ludlow," Sylvie said with a smile. "Our choices of books begin to look tired and few after a while."

"My pleasure," I said sincerely. "And please, call me Kate. Ready to go, Ellis?"

"Sure, Mom," Ellis said, walking to the other corner of the room to gather her things.

"How are you doing, Sylvie? Are you handling the loss of your brother, okay?" I noticed that Ellis hung back, going through her backpack, as if looking for something. She probably knew I was up to no good. Would she be understanding, or annoyed. With Ellis, or any teen girl, I imagine, it depended on the day and her mood.

Her eyes skidded to Ellis. "Does she? Do you have a minute?"

I held up a finger in a 'just a minute gesture.' "Hey, Elle, do you have a couple minutes to spare?"

I even got a smile. "Sure, Mom." I actually have to do some quick studying of *To Kill a Mockingbird.* I have a sneaking suspicion we are going to have a pop quiz in second-period English." She settled into the teacher's rocking chair, as if she had done so a million times.

People tend to tell me things. That, for some reason, I am perceived to be a good confidant. I really don't know why. I don't think it's that I look like a mom, because even people over the phone do it. I guess I come across as a kind, trustworthy person. If that's the case, it makes me happy.

Sylvie motioned me over to the area by her desk. She had an adult visitors' chair next to her desk. Must be time for parent/teacher conferences.

"I really appreciate you're asking, Mrs. ...Kate," She smiled self-consciously. "I don't really know who to talk to. My co-workers just brush it under the carpet, as if it's so uncomfortable, they pretend it didn't happen. Even my husband doesn't want to talk about it. He asks if I'm 'okay,' but changes the subject when I try to talk to him about my feelings."

Now I'm feeling awful. I wasn't really inquiring about her because I cared, but to get information. Poor young woman! What she must be going through.

But I'm a little embarrassed to say that didn't stop my scheming.

"I'm very sorry, Sylvie. What a wretched time this must be for you. Congratulations on your marriage, by the way. I'm a little surprised to see you at school. I thought you might take a wedding trip."

"We will go somewhere in the summer—when things calm down some." She looked down at her hands.

"Of course," I said softly. I knew it. "Have the police made any progress?" I knew they hadn't, but didn't know what else to say.

"Not really. I will be able to bury him soon. The funeral is next week. I hope you will be able to come."

"Oh yes, Ellis and I will be there." I placed my hand on hers that was resting on the desk and gave it a gentle squeeze. Her hands were so cold.

Now or never, I told myself. I took a breath. This insensitive side of myself wasn't one I really liked. "I know Clyde was dating Maria Di'Rissi, but they broke up?" I framed it as a question. She nodded. I don't think she trusted her voice; her eyes were full of tears.

"Was he seeing anyone new?" There, I did it, but not without disliking myself a little.

"Yes, he had just started seeing someone. In fact, my husband and I were going to get together with them for dinner. We had set something up, then…" the tears did roll down her almost baby cheeks then.

"So, you hadn't met her?"

She shook her head no. "What was her name? Can she help answer any questions? Help in any way?" I queried. I wondered if she'd call me out and ask me why I was so curious. But she was so sad, I don't think she noticed. I felt even more guilty.

"I don't even know her name," Sylvie responded in a hushed voice. "That just devastates me. I'd love to reach out. Maybe we could be some comfort to each other."

"Do you know where she worked? Any of their friends? Is she on social media?" I asked these questions in rapid-fire progression. I knew Ellis would have to go soon, and/or Sylvie would have to get her class from the art teacher. I knew I was overstepping.

"I guess I never thought of any of those things. I remember Clyde saying she did some modeling for some of his photos that he posted, I guess on Instagram. And I think she was a barista somewhere." That was all super helpful.

I felt that I had overstayed my welcome. But she was so gracious, she didn't make me feel bad. "I really should get Ellis to the high school for that pop quiz. Please know I'm thinking of you. If you ever want to talk again," I rummaged around in my cross-body pocketbook and pulled out one of my business cards. "The phone number on this card is my cell. Call anytime." And I meant it.

Chapter Thirty-three

Make sure your wedding planner coordinates with your ceremony musicians, be it live music or a DJ, so she knows when to tell the parents and bridal party to walk for the ceremony procession. The parents also need a heads-up on where to sit after they walk down the aisle.

After I dropped Ellis off at school with a 'good luck on the pop-quiz' wish, I drove to my office and parked behind the structure. It's rare that I drive to the office, but today it just made sense.

I went up the outside staircase, vs. the interior of The Perk. I didn't want to see anyone or chat today. I wanted to get to my computer and check out Clyde's Instagram. Was it even still up? Sometimes, family members took the social media accounts down after a loved one passed. I guess that would fall to Sylvie.

I opened Instagram on my laptop. I usually viewed the app and posted on my phone, but I needed a bigger picture. I went right to Clyde's page, and thank goodness, it was still up. I scrolled through his account and saw lots and lots of wedding photos. All the photos seemed to be clients, not models, or friends. But I kept looking, and I finally found someone who just might be the new girlfriend. She wasn't with a groom in any of her photos. The tags seemed to be advertising wedding products. **@prettymiss** very well could be her. When I clicked on her Instagram handle, I was taken to her page, but it was private. Dang! I requested her as a friend. While I waited to see if she responded, I decided to work on the timeline for the Webster wedding. I was a little concerned about the transportation schedule. If a wedding was going to have guest transportation, it was absolutely vital that the transportation be on time. If it was late, the whole event had the possibility of running late. And that was a recipe for disaster. A couple will still get married, still have their meal, but they may miss out on much of the party time. Most venues, as well as the entertainment, have a hard stop, meaning you must end on time.

Jessie Webster, the bride in question, didn't want her guests waiting overlong at the church for the ceremony to start, but she also didn't want to pay for two buses. She had so many guests to transport that she either needed two buses or one bus had to make two trips. She wanted to cut it too close to the ceremony start time. We were going to need to have a talk. I was putting it off, but it would have to be done soon, as the bus times couldn't be changed after this week. I kept looking at my phone. Nothing yet from **@prettymiss**. Uuuuuugggg. I threw my head down on my desk in despair. I almost slammed my laptop lid down; I was too conscious of the cost to really slam it down. I stood up and grabbed my pocketbook. I'd take a break and go see who was downstairs at The Perk.

I skipped down the stairs. I never fail to be thankful to do so after my injury. I gripped my phone in a death hold. I could hardly wait to get downstairs to check to see if **@prettymiss** had accepted my friend request. I went to my usual table. I scanned the bar for Jen. I didn't initially see her at this time of day, but then she popped her head out from the kitchen area, her gloved hands covered in dough. Jen smiled but was obviously busy. I had frequently told her she needed to farm out her baking, but she loved it, so...

I woke my phone up and refreshed the Instagram app. No new friends for me. I thought most young people were always on their socials! It had been an hour and a half. Maybe she just wasn't going to accept me.

I felt the draft of the front door of the coffee shop opening. And there was Sarah, sauntering in as only Sarah can. Today, she was all glammed out. She must have had a closing or something off-site. She was dressed in a navy sheath dress of what could only be silk. She had paired it with a wide brown belt, which accentuated her small waist. She wore brown Penelope Chilvers tall boots, you know, the ones like Catherine, the Princess of Wales, still wears, left over from her university days? The ones with the tassels on the side zipper? Her pocketbook was a mini-Kelly in gold on gold. If I knew anything about Sarah, it was the real deal. At a minimum of thirty to forty thousand dollars, that bag was well out of *my* reach—but then so were the seven-hundred-dollar boots.

Sarah tossed down her light-as-a-feather deep green cashmere dress coat on the chair next to me and asked, "Want anything from the coffee bar or bakery case?"

"No thanks," I answered. If I had any more caffeine today, I'd be a danger to those around me.

Sarah joined me with a take-out coffee cup and…a super large brownie.

"What the heck, Sarah?" I felt my eyes bug out. "Are you really going to eat that?"

She broke off a big chunk of the brownie. "Well, at least half of it. I closed a massive deal today, and this is my reward."

Worked for me. I joined her in breaking off a bite, although not as large as hers. I knew I wouldn't be hitting the gym the way I was sure she would be today.

"What's up, Manet?" Sarah said around her brownie chewing.

I rehashed my visit with Sylvie, and my plan to 'friend' **@prettymiss**, and share her Instagram handle.

"How long has it been since you requested to be friends?"

I looked at my watch. "About two hours now."

Sarah shook her head. "She's not going to accept your friend request, Katie. These kids, they are on their socials twenty-four/seven. If she hasn't accepted you by now, she's not going to." She fiddled with her phone, opening Instagram, I was sure. She typed away. "There," she said.

"What did you do?" I asked.

"Seeing if she'll take the bait. Sarah took a sip of her coffee. She must be wearing one of those new lip stain things. No color was left on her white paper cup, but her lips remained the most perfect rosy shade. Ellis and her friends were all trying it. I rounded the corner one day from the great room to the kitchen and saw a trio of girls with black lips. Apparently, you paint that on your lips, let it dry, then peel it off to perfectly stained lips that last for hours. Add a lip plumper on top. and one doesn't have to get filler…or so I hear.

"What bait," I wondered.

"I have a fake Instagram account. I look like a twenty something from NYC, hip—the right clothes, great vacations, jacked boyfriend. You'd be surprised at the girls that trust me, and then I can snoop and do real estate research." She looked off. Was that a little bit of color in her cheeks?

"You just like to be the voyeur, Sarah. See what the young people are doing, admit it." I teased her.

She rolled her eyes at me, then said, "Ah ha! **@prettymiss** and I are friends."

I tried to grab Sarah's phone in my disbelief, but she was quicker than I. That was rude of me; I knew better than to touch another woman's phone.

"Are you kidding me?" Maybe she *did* know what she was doing. And I imagine a lot of Gen Z research could be done via Instagram. Kudos, Sarah, I thought. "Scoot around here, Katie," She moved out the chair next to her. I plopped down in it and leaned over to look at her phone. **@Prettymiss** was a very pretty girl. I looked up her profile information, but she had no name attached. Odd—but not unheard of.

"Any clues as to where she works? Clyde's sister says she may be a barista. Sarah widened her eyes at me and looked around.

I rolled my eyes back at her.

"I'm looking," Sarah shot back at me. "Looks like she's a barista at Jen's competition, Starbucks, and one in town." We actually had two Starbucks in Eastbury, but I had never set foot in either. Looks like I would today.

I stood up and grabbed my pocketbook. I didn't have a sweater with me, but I'd live. I *could* go back upstairs and grab the emergency one I kept in my office, but I didn't want to.

"Are you coming?" I said over my shoulder to Sarah.

"Wouldn't miss it," she stood up and put on her beautiful coat. "Aren't you going to be cold? Where's your sweater?"

"I'll be alright, *Mom*," I said with a giggle.

"I'll drive," she said as her come back.

By mutual agreement, we drove to the Starbucks closest to Jen's, the Huron Avenue store. She parked in the lot; the store was part of a planned grouping of shops that wasn't older than three years. Most of the long-time Eastbury residents had strong feelings about the development of our tiny burg. You either loved the growth…or hated it. I was a fan, as the more people here, the more who got married.

We didn't know her name, so we couldn't ask if this was her assigned store, and even if we found she worked at this location, we couldn't ask if she was working today. It would be too weird if we showed her picture and asked around about her. Fingers crossed she worked at this location, and she was on today.

Sarah opened the door for me at Starbucks, and we queued up in line. There were only two people ahead of us, and I didn't know either one. I hope they were out of towners. Otherwise, they were cheating on our hometown girl, Jen, and her shop. I looked around hungrily, it's not that I've never been to a Starbucks before, I used to go all the time when we lived in California. But I haven't been to one since we moved here. The only reason was that Jen's shop was everything—good coffee, food, community, and…Jen. As we waited in line, I looked at the offerings in the bakery case and baskets scattered around the coffee bar. No wonder Jen baked like crazy. All the Starbucks baked goods were the same everywhere: same muffins, scones, breads, egg bites, etc. Jen had a rolling change of menu. She toyed with her customers, surprising and delighting them with her daily changes. It was one of the reasons she had returning daily customers, to see what the specials were. When I really thought about it, it was a darn good marking system.

It was finally our turn to order, and the barista wasn't **@prettymiss.** Sarah ordered for both of us, just a tall hot coffee with room for cream, although I doubted Sarah would splurge on the cream. Sigh, neither would I.

"I think my sister said my nephew's new love interest works here," Sarah said in a conspiring tone to the barista taking her payment. "My sis showed me a picture, but I don't see anyone who looks like her." Sarah looked over the barista's shoulder to the two girls working the drive-thru and the barista making the drinks.

Our barista raised one pierced eyebrow at us. "What's her name? We have other staff who are off today or working second shift. Are you even sure she works at this location?" You could tell she was ready to move on to the customer behind us. I can't say I blamed her. I went to get a table, and Sarah hung around the bakery case, and went back to the barista after the couple behind us was helped.

Sarah asked for a piece of lemon cake. I saw her speaking softly to the barista, but I couldn't hear her. Then she came back smiling

"I described **@prettymiss**, and she works at the other location. Let's go." I picked up my coffee and took a big gulp; I burnt my tongue.

Chapter Thirty-four

Your bar: will you have a full bar with cocktails or just a beer and wine bar? If you can, I advise purchasing the alcohol yourself. But many venues and caterers do not allow this. Some states have very restrictive liquor laws. You can save a big chunk of money if you serve only beer and wine. If you go this route, I advise that you have no offerings of hard liquor. Some couples offer complimentary beer and wine, then ask their guests to pay for cocktails. This is an uncomfortable situation for all.

If I had to drink one more cup of coffee, I'd float away. I had already declined a cup at Jen's, and here I was drinking two more cups at two different Starbucks. But when we arrived at Eastbury's second Starbucks location, I knew I'd have to order something. I was starting to get a little hungry and thought maybe I'd order a couple of sandwiches for Ellis and me to eat for dinner. I opened the door for Sarah this time, and we both entered the shop. And there she was, **@prettymiss**. She wasn't taking orders, but the barista was making the drinks. Sarah sent me a side-eyed message…' what?' I wanted to ask. We were getting along pretty well, but I couldn't read her mind.

There was no line at this location, and Sarah stepped right up and ordered us two Grande cappuccinos. Oh, I get it. If we had ordered just hot coffees, the barista taking the orders would serve it to us. But with the specialty drinks, we could maybe interact with **@prettymiss**.

Sarah paid, thanks Sarah! I grabbed a table, which was no great feat, the store was almost empty.

"Sarah," **@prettymiss** called out. We looked at each other. Who was going to go up? I rose, and Sarah remained seated. I blew a big breath out. I wasn't sure what to say, what to ask.

I walked up to the 'coffee pick up' section and smiled at **@prettymiss**. "Thanks," I said as I picked up our drinks. She smiled back. Nice teeth, I thought.

"Oh, may I please have about four packets of 'Sugar in the Raw,'" I asked politely. She turned to grab them, and when she did, I widened my eyes in horror as a thought occurred to me. What if she recognized me from my Instagram photo when I requested to follow her? My photo was a headshot that one of my photographer friends did for me free of charge. It was a good pic, and I used it on everything. Maybe she hadn't been on her socials as she was working, but she *did* accept Sarah's request, so I guess she had been on...I grabbed the sugar and scurried back to my seat.

"What's wrong, Manet?" Sarah called me out on my weird behavior right away.

"I didn't even think. What if she recognizes me from my Instagram request?"

"You use your real photo?

"Of course, I use my real photo. It's my business account!" I hissed back.

"Okay, okay!" Sarah said, all defensive, holding her hands up in a surrender pose. "I'll go talk to her and try to suss some information out. Any particular questions you want me to ask?"

Oh Jeeze. I hadn't thought that far. I initially wanted to find her. I also wanted to know if she had any suspects in the death of Clyde...could she be one? Although she didn't look like someone who had archery expertise. But did Addalee? Looks can be deceiving. Addalee had had a series of stepfathers/uncles. Most were bad guys. But one...what was his name? had been a pretty decent man. He liked to hunt and fish with his misfit/makeshift family. Addalee showed an interest, so he took her hunting with him quite often. He taught her to use a compound bow. I remember Addalee missing school when it was the beginning of a new hunting season. Addie got quite good, and it was nice to see her have something she felt proud of. This led to some tournaments, where she also excelled. Sadly, this nice guy was killed by a drunk driver when she was seventeen. I don't know how she would have gotten through that loss if he hadn't been for Cory, her then boyfriend, now husband.

"Got it," Sarah said, pulling me out of my memories. "Stick your nose in your phone. She is actually looking over here," I started to look up. Don't look, Manet, Jeeze." The irritation was heavy on Sarah's face as she walked back to the coffee bar.

I tried not to look at Sarah and **@prettymiss** but couldn't help myself. I snuck a glance here and there. Sarah and **@prettymiss** seemed to be getting on like a house on fire. Then I saw Sarah pull out a business card from her crossbody bag. They smiled at each other, and Sarah came back.

I tried not to look too eager, but I don't think I was successful. "What happened? Did you get her name? Did you learn anything?"

Sarah pulled out her chair and pressed her palm down toward the table in a slowdown motion. "Take a breath, Katie." She scolded.

I did take a breath and waited. Sarah seemed to enjoy my discomfort.

"Good news or bad news first?" Sarah asked.

"There's bad news already? You just met her!" Sarah frowned.

"She recognized you," Sarah shared.

"No!" I said with honest surprise.

"Yep," she leaned back in a relaxed, yet gleeful pose. Hey, weren't we on the same page? She shouldn't be happy at my discomfort.

"So, what's the good news?" I was ready for some good news.

"Her break is in five minutes, and she's willing to talk to us." Sarah smiled, that Deloro smug self-satisfied smile that I *hated*. Same team, Katie, same team, I reminded myself.

"Good job," I heard myself say.

We were quiet for the five minutes **@prettymiss** requested, but we were both getting fidgety.

Finally, **@prettymiss** lifted the bar separating the baristas from the dining area, took off her apron, and joined us. She carried what looked like the Starbucks 'pink drink.'

"You wanted to talk to me," she said as a way of intro, as she pulled a chair to sit at our table. The chair dragged on the floor, making a horrific screeching noise.

Sarah looked to me. "Yes, I said. I'm Katie, and this is Sarah."

"Sarah, I met, but you," she took a gulp of her pink drink. "You're a stalker." This last was said with no emotion, as she pointed to me with her cup. This made me feel creepy and icky.

She was mute in my discomfort. Sarah came to my rescue. "We're not going for the ick effect," Sarah tried to smile warmly, but couldn't quite pull it off. She looked…weird.

Time for me to pick up the slack.

"Sorry about that," I looked her right in the eye. "I knew Clyde, and I recently found out the two of you had started seeing each other. I wanted to say how sorry we," I motioned between Sarah and me, "were, and ask a couple questions."

@prettymiss leaned back in her chair and stretched out her long legs. She had a brown pixie haircut that was frosted at the tips, which she gelled into spikes, and more piercings than I could count: her nose, several in her ears, her eyebrow; but it worked for her. Her beauty was delicate and somehow wholesome.

"Who are you again? I know you've been checking out my Insta," she looked at me here, "but *why* are you *really* here?"

Well, this was awkward. She wasn't going to make this easy on me. "I'm a wedding planner, and I worked with Clyde. He was a great photographer. I'm sorry for your loss." I used my mom voice. "I don't think I asked your name."

@prettymiss's head jerked up. "You know I was seeing Clyde, but you don't know my name. You found me here at my place of employment, but you don't know my name?"

I was silent. Not sure if it would work, but…I saw Sarah begin to crack. She was going to say something. I shot her a look, and she closed her mouth.

"Missy," she said softly, looking over my shoulder. "My name's Melissa, but everyone calls me Missy." She said with a little more volume and definite eye contact this time.

Ah, that makes sense of her Instagram handle. "Cute Insta handle," I said.

This earned me a genuine smile, and she was radiant. Her whole face lit up with that smile. "Thanks." She had the most endearing chip on her front tooth It made her look younger than she probably was.

"We hadn't been seeing each other for long. It was really chill, we'd just hang out, stream some shows, get takeout. Sometimes, I'd even help him on some of his photo gigs. He even posted pics of me on his socials." She looked wistful, then sad.

"Do you know of anyone who he had a beef with? Was anyone angry with *him*?" Sarah asked.

I watched Missy closely. I saw her swallow, as if she was preparing herself. "You know, usually in situations like this, the friend/family member says, 'No, everyone *loved* him!' But that wasn't the way it was with Clyde. He had more enemies than anyone I ever knew, and there weren't many people he liked. He was always getting into it with work associates, clients, and his bosses. I can only imagine how long the list of suspects would be with him. He was cool with me, because he was into me, but he wasn't nice to most people. Sometimes I wondered why I liked him. I guess because he was a bad ass."

This really wasn't helpful. So, we now have lots more suspects than when we walked in the door. I looked around Starbucks. The place almost gave me a hospital vibe, with everything so utilitarian. Jen did such a better job of décor. Her shop was warm, this was…not.

Missy brought me back to the conversation. "I wish I could help you; I want justice for Clyde. I just don't know if I know anything. The only thing that happened out of the ordinary before he died was that last night, he got a call that made him mad, really mad. I was in the bathroom, and didn't know he was on the phone until I came out. He was speaking to whoever with anger and in threatening tones. It was a different call than I've heard him on before. I've seen him be a jerk, joke, and be disrespectful, but never threatening. He saw me standing there and said, "I've got to go." I asked him what that was all about, and he tried to blow it off, saying it was nothing, when it was obvious that it was something.

"What time was this, Missy?" I asked. She scrunched up to face in thought.

"Probably about 10:30 PM. The thing that struck me was the threatening tone of his voice, as well as his words He said, 'don't mess with me, or your sweet Violet will hear about it. And we both know you don't want that."

Sweet Violet, I thought. Well, it was something. Did I know any Violets? We thanked Missy and took our leave.

"What do you think?" Sarah asked as we climbed into her Range Rover.

"I think we need to look for someone named Violet."

Chapter Thirty-five

Will you write your own vows? If so, do it early in your wedding prep. There is nothing worse than trying to compose something heartfelt under pressure. When it comes time for the big day, don't forget to take your notes to the ceremony! It's a good idea to have either your maid of honor or your best man hold those vows. Never a good idea to use your phone for this. I know we all use them for notes, but this is not the time or the place.

After Sarah dropped me off at home, I deposited the Starbucks sandwiches in the fridge and went to my home office. Not much had been gleaned from Missy, but she had given me the name Violet. It seemed important because Clyde was speaking to someone he had issues with when he mentioned her.

Instagram had been good to me when it came to the sleuthing department. I plopped into my Costco office chair behind my desk and opened up my laptop. I went to the Instagram app and was ready to dig in when I heard Ellis come in through the mud room door.

"Hey, Mom, Ellis bellowed.

"I'm in my office," I responded.

Then Ellis filled my oversized doorway—remember, my office is a former twin parlor, so there are no closed doors, just an opening. She was magnificent. Her long chestnut hair was down. She must have pulled the ponytail holder off when she got home. I know for a fact she can't stand to have her hair down when she's playing sports. She was dressed in sweats and an old t-shirt, and I don't know when my girl had looked more beautiful.

She oozed health and vitality. And she smelled...like sunshine.

"Did you run outside?" I asked, noting the sunshine smell and her rosy cheeks.

"How did you know?" she asked, surprised.

I can smell the autumn coming off you," I smiled, and she smiled back. I truly don't think there is a more beautiful sight.

"I have some things to finish up here, but I'll join you in a bit—I bought sandwiches from Starbucks, they're in the frig—guessing you want to shower?"

Ellis rolled her eyes at me. "I think I better. First you say you can smell the Autumn coming off me, then you ask if I'm going to shower."

I laughed. "You know it's not that."

"I don't know, Mom. You are usually very direct." Ah, she was in a good mood. Nothing better. She ran upstairs, and I continued to Instagram.

I went to my page and the search bar. I typed in 'Violet.' All kinds of things came up. Nothing seemed to mean anything to me. Then I checked my notifications. **@prettymiss** had accepted my friend request. Will wonders never cease? I scrolled through her feed, but nothing jumped out at me. I had seen most of it from Sarah's account.

I went to Facebook next. I looked through my friend list. I had about three thousand friends, so you never know...But once again, nothing.

Chapter Thirty-Six

There is nothing wrong with tried-and-true traditions in wedding scenarios. They are tried-and-true for a reason; they work. So often, couples try to be different and innovative. One time, I had a groom make his entrance via a helicopter. He thought he hung the moon, and it was impressive, but it did take away from the bride. And even though it's the couple's day, it is MORE the bride's than anyone's.

Another meeting with Charlie and Remley. It would be my first with Remley since the 'shut up' incident. And yes, it had been quite a while since all three of us had met. I hadn't the stomach for an interaction.

We were once again meeting in my office. Charlie, always the peacemaker, had insisted on bringing treats. He said he was dropping by the Italian district of Hartford and getting the goodies from Modern Pastry. I loved that shop.

Charlie and Remley entered from the outside stairs with the cold breeze of fall. Their cheeks were ruddy with cold and health. They were laughing as they entered and seemed to be in high spirits.

Remley was wearing a suede shearling coat, on my 'to die for' wish list, brown Chelsea boots, a short green corduroy skirt, and the cutest olive-green beret and matching gloves. Her hair looked to be freshly cut and blown out. Her make-up was just right—with that trending "French Girl no-make-up" make-up. She had come loaded for bear.

I was no slacker. I wore a Tencel fabric shirt dress in deep blues with tights and my Penelope Chivers tall brown tassel boots, yes, I had ordered them after coveting Sarah's—quite the splurge for me. I had taken extra time with my hair today, and had my own version of French Girl no make-up, you can also read that, no make-up, but I felt good. The best armor is feeling good in your own skin.

As they entered my tiny reception area, I greeted them warmly and with smiles.

"Good morning," I enthused. They responded in kind, and Charlie handed me a pink bakery box, all tied up with white string. I accepted it with a sunny thank you and beckoned them into my inner office. I had set up coffee service, complete with china coffee pot, creamer and sugar, as well as plates and cheery little napkins with violets on them. You know my favorite flower, and now a mystery name.

We settled in chairs around the coffee table (so much more friendly than around my desk) and I opened the bakery box. It revealed a variety of breakfast cake slices, muffins, scones, and rolls. My mouth watered. I went to my mini kitchen/hostess area and grabbed a tiered display dish to plate the goodies on.

I was happy to see that Remley and Charlie dug into the pastries enthusiastically. They were less likely to notice I was abstaining. I was really trying to eat better. I poured coffee and remembered they both took it black. Finally, we were ready to discuss the wedding.

"Well, first of all, I want to say again how sorry I am for the loss of Clyde. I know you were friends." I thought it would be better to skip the fact that I knew Clyde was her cousin.

Remley looked down at her coffee cup and gave a whispered, "Thanks."

I paused, allowing for some respect for Clyde. Then, I said, "Have you thought about a replacement photographer? I have referral names with contact information if you're interested.

Remley remained silent, but Charlie said, "Thanks, Katie. That would be great."

"I'll email the list over to you this afternoon. Are there any other holes in your vendor list? If so, just let me know and I'll send those names, numbers, and emails along as well." Remley was still silent, all her previous blustery joy gone.

Charlie took a big bite of scone. He picked up a napkin. Look, Rem, violets." Charlie said around his big bite. "Violet is my pet name for Remley."

Remley smiled coyly, and I felt my face blanch.

Chapter Thirty-seven

Charlie and Remley left amid giggles and kisses. I sat quietly at my desk after they were gone. 'Violet'! Charlie's pet name for Remley was 'Violet?' Could it possibly be the Violet from Clyde's rantings that Missy heard when he was on the phone?

I stumbled down the stairs to Jen's and took a seat at my usual table, ignoring Tally's wave of greeting. This whole thing was a mess. It served me right for not keeping my nose out of all of this. I had no business in the murder investigation. I had helped prove Addalee innocent; that should be enough.

"Hey, Vi, grab me another muffin when you're up there," shouted a customer. 'Vi' as in Violet? I smiled and shook myself. Oh, Jeeze. I was overreacting.

I had about thirty minutes before I had to be at 'First Bloom,' the florist chosen for my wedding in two weeks. The bride was…a little much. She wanted to change her color scheme, which was okay with the florist, but the flowers she wanted now were not in season. Not only was it iffy if the florist would be able to obtain them, but the price would also naturally go up. Wedding tip—choose in-season flowers for the best value. I headed out of Jen's, thinking how best to have my florist's back with her concerns and at the same time have my bride's. I wanted her to be happy without stretching her pocketbook too far. I pulled the door open to First Bloom. Oh, good, my bride wasn't here yet. And Mandy, the florist, must be in the back. I had just made myself at home at the bistro table and chairs when my phone pinged with an incoming text. I pulled my phone from the outside pocket of my bag and nervously saw it was from Remley.

Katie, I sort of avoided offering more of an apology about the whole 'shut up' incident than I should have. What do you say we meet up at our new house for a glass of wine. I'd really like to make it up to you, and at the same time pick your brain about a new photographer.

Oh, Jeeze. I did *not* want to do this, but I didn't see a way out of it.

Sure Remley, I'd love that. What time?

Five-thirty. Can't wait!

* * *

When I drove up to Remley and Charlie's new house, I knew instantly that I was in love with it. The grounds were exquisite. The sun was going down, and I bet the landscaping was even more impressive under a sparkling blue sky. I parked in the circular drive and made my way to the massive front door. All the lights were already on in the beautiful white colonial, but the front door was slightly ajar. I rang the bell, but no one came. I decided to walk in, as I was an invited guest, and I had been known to leave my own door ajar if I was expecting guests but had to run down to the basement or up the stairs for a moment and didn't want to miss my guests.

"Hello," I called out. And that was all she wrote. All went black, and I can only assume I went down.

I awoke to the feel of a cold floor and my hands bound. Cuffs, if I wasn't mistaken. I had to get out of them. I felt panic rise. If I didn't, I was done for. What had I seen recently on TikTok? It was a video tutorial on how to get out of handcuffs. I was cuffed to a pillar with my hands behind. I took a step back and put one foot over the chain between my hands, and then stepped over the chain with the other foot. Whoa! It worked. My yoga exercises were paying off. My hands were now in front of me! Okay. Could I pull off the second step, that of getting the cuffs off without a key? I'd sure try. I had no other choice, not if I wanted to live. For surely the person who had cuffed me and thrown me wherever I was wasn't playing. I pulled off the scarf, which I had casually wrapped as an accessory around my neck that morning; weird as scarf-wearing wasn't my thing. Can you say intuition? The scarf was a gift from an appreciative bride. It was made from the lightest of silk, fragile like butterfly wings. Beautiful, yes, but sturdy? I didn't know. The color was to die for, though. Sure, hope I wasn't going to…

Step two. I untied the scarf and pulled it from my neck. I used a simple noose knot, (thanks Mom and Dad for insisting I take those sailing lessons), at one end of the scarf, then wove the other end around and around the bracelet of the cuff covering it. I focused mainly on the part of the cuff that had the hinge, which opened the cuff. I then squatted down and put my foot in the loop I had created with the knot on the scarf. I put gentle tension on the scarf, while trying to scrunch my fingers into my hand as small as I could, while continuing to put pressure on my foot in the scarf loop. That sweet scarf was pretty darn strong. Pull, pull, pull, ouch, ouch, ouch. The video tutorial didn't say anything about how much this would hurt. Dang! And then, it was off. I looked at the makeshift contraption in disbelief. Did this really just happen? Okay, I still had one cuff on, and it was inconvenient, but hey, I could get out of this room. Or so I thought. Yep, the door was securely locked from the outside. Well, I'd just have to break a window. I looked around to see what I could use to accomplish this. I had been so focused on my plight of being handcuffed to a support beam, I had not surveyed my surroundings. Now I did. Who was this weirdo who had *nothing*, and I mean *nothing* in their garage? When I say nothing, I'm not kidding. But if this was Charlie and Remley's house, and they were just moving in, I guess it made sense. Either they didn't have garage stuff, or it hadn't arrived yet. Yes, there were windows on the right side of the garage, but they were very high. The garage ceiling wasn't your typical height. I bet it was a good twenty feet high. The windows were almost to the ceiling, so no way was I breaking out of them. I looked around me. The idiot had left my purse. Was my cell phone inside? I scooped my purse like a marathon runner grabbing a paper cup of water from a volunteer. I looked down at my wrist as I dove into my purse. My Apple Watch was gone. Of course, they had taken my phone. But I had my purse. Oh, what a mistake they had made...I all but cackled to myself.

Now to find the perfect rocket to throw against the garage window. I rummaged around my Louis "Never full" and discarded my eyeglasses case, toiletry case (maybe this would work if all else failed), and a full water bottle. This would be a last resort. I think I'd keep it as long as I could for hydration. In fact, I opened it and took a big swig. I put my hand back in my purse, rooting around. Then my fingers landed on it. I loved my portable phone charger. It had saved my bacon on more than one occasion when my cell phone was close to dying. Maybe it would save me today.

First, I wanted to see if I could hear anything outside. I trotted over to the middle garage door bay and placed my ear to the door, straining to hear any sign of life. Nothing. I kept at it for at least ten minutes, and then I heard what sounded like a truck blowing its horn. You know the real loud one where the driver has to pull the chain, and it explodes with a deep hooonk hoooonk? Well, that's what I remember as a kid. Not sure if that's how it worked anymore, but that's what it sounded like. And it appeared from what sounded like the crunching of gravel that the truck was pulling into the drive. Okay, I was going to hurl my cell phone portable charger at one of these windows (how could I miss?), and when it crashed through the window, the truck driver would investigate. A perfect plan! He must be making a delivery for some sort of heavy equipment or something. Why so late? It was almost dark out now. What did I care? I aimed for the middle window; that way, if I was slightly off, it would hit one of the windows on either side. I went right between the second and third window. What the heck? I tried again and missed...again. My charger clattered to the garage floor and shattered this time. I ran to pick it up, cradling it like I would an injured baby bird. I tried to snap the back onto the front again. It worked, kinda. I think I had one more shot before this thing fell apart. And then I heard it. The honk honk of the truck's horn, and the beep, beep, beep indicating it was in reverse and leaving. Crap. No, no, NO! Don't leave me. In my desperation, I hurled the phone charger as hard as I could, and I somehow smashed through window number two. And it was impressive. The window must not have been tempered, because it shattered spectacularly. Not a good choice, homeowner.

The beep beep beep of the truck's reverse gear stopped. So did the crunch on the gravel. The truck had heard me! Now, I would find out if the driver was friend or foe, probably something I should have thought about before I hurled my trusty charger out that window. But I really didn't have any other choice.

I pushed my ear against the garage door again and listened.

"Hello?' Someone pounded on the aluminum garage door, and I thought my head would explode. Ouch! But I didn't wait long.

"Help! Help!" I screamed at the top of my lungs.

The voice came right next to me on the other side of the door, "Are you stuck in there?"

"I'm a prisoner, more like it. Can you get me out?"

"A prisoner! He shouted, putting my fears to rest that he was in cahoots with my captor. Well, I can try the access door," (a regular door like any other, on the side of the garage with the windows, not a roll-up garage door).

I heard him stomp around to the access door and rattle and slam into the door, but it didn't budge.

That's when I heard it, the crack of the rifle shot. And what sounded like a body slumping into the door. Oh my God! What just happened? Was my savior just shot? Are you kidding me? Real terror gripped my heart.

I pressed my ear, this time to the access door. I could hear moans. "Are you okay?" I stupidly asked the man on the other side of the door. Of course, he wasn't okay. Dollars to donuts, he was shot. Oh my God! I could be responsible for this poor man's death. At least he was moaning.

"Don't worry, you're going to be okay. I'll get help." I think I almost heard a chuckle.

"Now how you going to do that, Little Lady?" He said softly.

Little Lady? Get a grip, Manet, I scolded myself. And yes, I knew I sounded like Sarah.

"He just got me in the shoulder, but I'm not real mobile. I'm going to play dead, so don't rat me out. He's on his way down here."

"It's a he?" I had to ask

"Just a way of takin' Little Lady. Couldn't see who was firing the shot, but...quiet now."

I heard the heavy steps approach. Sounded like a man, but maybe a heavy woman? I heard what sounded like someone kicking flesh, as in the poor man in front of the door. Then it sounded like someone was pulling my would-be savior away from the access door. I gulped.

The door opened with a stereotypical creak, like one of those old horror movies. And a man, yes, he was a man, walked in. My gaze went up from his motorcycle boots to jeans and shirt, and leather jacket to his...mask. Well darn. All I can say is that it was probably good for me that he was masked. That meant that he was going to let me live, right? If he didn't have that rifle in his right hand, I'd rush him and try out some of my new personal defense moves. Yeah, right, who was I kidding? I was no match against his bulk—and his rifle.

So, I did what any self-respecting woman would do who didn't want to die. I ran to the far corner of the garage, he rushed me, but I was faster. I faked left and went right. I was like the puppy my parents gave me when I was ten years old. He was tiny, but when he didn't want to be caught because he knew he was going in his crate, there wasn't much anyone could do to catch him. But I wasn't a puppy, and there wasn't furniture for me to hide behind. With minimal effort, the masked one caught me. He wrapped his left arm around my middle and lifted me off the ground one-handed. I kicked my feet back at him, but he just held me away from him. Well, that wasn't going to do much good. Was he going to shoot me? I shopped, kicking my feet. Maybe it was in my best interest to settle down and try to negotiate with him. Or...I reached behind me and pulled his mask off. If I was going to die, I wanted to see my executioner. I turned around and looked at my attacker's face.

Oh...my...God. It was Charlie. CHARLIE! He set me down, and I turned toward him, and if I thought about it, I would have thought that intruders had entered Charlie and Remley's new home, and this was one of the 'bad guys.'

I was breathless. "Charlie," I whispered.

And then he did the most surprising thing. He leaned down and placed a gentle, but not brotherly kiss right on my lips. I let him linger there as my body was coming to terms with what my brain knew to be true. It was Charlie!

"I had to do that, just once, he said before I saw the butt of the rife lift—and then darkness.

I awoke again in the back of Charlie's Suburban. I hit my poor head again on the side of the cargo area, ouch! I knew better this time not to alert Charlie that I was conscious. We bumped along a few minutes more, then came to a gradual stop. Charlie turned off the engine. I heard his driver's side door open, then close. I heard him walking outside the truck to the back, where I was stowed. What was he going to do with me? Would Charlie really kill me? If that was his plan, why didn't he do it in the garage? Because it would be too much of a mess to clean up, the rational side of my brain answered. 'And how about that kiss?' The emotional side asked. Weird! The rational part answered. Yeah, all of me agreed. I knew he always had a little thing for me. Would that keep him from killing me? I rather doubted it. When it came down to Charlie or me, Charlie would pick himself every time. How the heck as I going to get out of this jam? Oh my! What about that poor truck driver? I had great hopes that he would call 911 and be saved, but let's face it. Probably not...

Charlie lifted the tailgate. "Rise and shine, Katie." Charlie's mask was off, but he didn't look like Charlie. His eyes looked a little scary, and even when he was looking right at me, it was as if he was looking through me. My goose was cooked.

He must be Clyde's killer, but why? I still hadn't put all the pieces together.

Charlie reached in and pulled me toward the opening of the back of the truck. "Time to take a little walk, Katie." He smiled, but the smile didn't reach his eyes.

And then my body took over my brain, and I kicked him in the face as he pulled me out. He fell back and shook his head in confusion, and I hope, pain.

Then I saw something I had never really seen on Charlie's face: anger, and he was raging.

"Why, you little snot!" He said menacingly, his face crimson, the hair around his face was curling with the moisture of his sweat. It wasn't hot out, but he seemed in distress, good! He tried to grab my feet, but I scooted out of his way and over the back of the third row of seats. He ran to the driver's side to open it and hopefully get me out the hard way. I locked the door on my way over into the front seats and scrambled to the passenger seat and out the door. Now we had something to run around, like my puppy and I when I was ten.

We appeared to be in some sort of forest, out by Cotton Hallow, our town's answer to a Lovers Lane. It didn't look familiar, but we could be back in some off-trail area. I bent down and picked up a baseball bat-sized piece of wood. I now had a weapon. Then I scooted under the Suburban. Charlie didn't see me do it. He ran around the truck looking frantic. I could see the wheels in his brain turning. How did I get away so fast? I scrambled out the other side and crept behind him. He must have heard me, because he started to turn, and that's when I conked him on the head with my make-shift bat, hard. He fell like a sack of rocks. Oh crap. Did I kill him? Not that he didn't deserve it, but I didn't *want* to kill him.

I had to make fast work of my rescue. I dug into Charlie's back pocket, ewww…and pulled out his cell. I held it up to his face, and it opened. I've often said there was a reason I didn't enable this feature on my phone. No one was opening *my* phone. I wasn't doing the fingerprint thing either. I didn't fancy someone cutting off one of my fingers to open my phone and keep access to it. Okay…I'll agree I watch too many dark movies. But they give me good ideas, right?

"911, what's your emergency?' The voice asked. That's when I crashed. Oh my God! What had just happened? Had I just cracked a tree branch over the head of one of my oldest friends? Was said friend guilty of murder?

I sobbed out my name and location and what had just happened. It took me three tries, but it wasn't five minutes before I heard the sirens of my cavalry, and Brian was in the front car.

He pulled into the area with a cloud of dust. He must have found me on the Find my Friends feature on his iPhone (that is, if Charlie had my phone with him), as I was off road. But find me, he did. He pulled me into his embrace, and then the waterworks flowed. I couldn't stop crying, in part because of the adrenaline, part for the loss of a friend. No, he wasn't dead. I had checked in my five-minute wait, but he was no longer my friend.

Chapter Thirty-eight

This is for the wedding party: The wedding day is the day to not be yourself. Always late? Don't be today; be early. Overly critical? Don't be today: be positive. Distractable, don't pay attention? Today, listen to direction. You will have your day, and you can run it as you wish.

I was able to sit behind the two-way mirror during Charlie's interview with the police. He didn't ask for an attorney, as he was one. Mistake. He revealed that Remley wasn't actually Clyde's cousin. He just said that so I would get off his trail. He also shared that he had used her phone to lure me to his house to 'get rid of me.' I should have realized when I read that text that Remley wouldn't call me 'Katie,' but then I never expected my longtime friend Charlie to try to kill me. He didn't want to kill me; it was just necessary, he said. He was doing some dirty business for Mr. Di'Rissi, and he didn't want the town to know that Good Boy Charlie was not such a good boy. He cherished his town rep. Clyde was always hanging out at the Di'Rissi estate because of Maria, and overheard some nasty dealings. Clyde thought Charlie was ripe for the picking to blackmail. He thought it was his chance to make a little money on the side. Charlie also said, with a laugh, that he had bought the bow and arrow at a tag sale and only practiced a little. But he was quite proud of his kill shot with Clyde. Did I ever know this man?

Chapter Thirty-nine

It's a great idea to visit your venue in the season you will be married. For example, if you book your event in the fall, but plan to be married in the spring, go visit the venue as soon as the spring leaves pop out, and you can get a good vision of what it will look like.

To say that I was nervous wouldn't even begin to describe the emotion I was feeling. Was I marching into my own execution? Would I ever be seen again? Sarah had assured me that it was a benign meeting, that I had nothing to fear. Really? I was taking life advice, and I mean *life* advice…from Sarah Deloro? I told both Sarah and Brian that if I didn't contact them both in an hour, they were to come to the Di'Rissi estate with guns blazing.

I made my way to the exclusive conclave of estates on top of the hill in Eastbury. These estates had the most magnificent views of Hartford, and they had the 'view tax' to prove it. The gates to the estate were open, and I drove my Suburban through them and up to the house via the circular drive. Should I park right in front of the door? I didn't have to wonder long. A gardener, decked out in jeans, a green long-sleeved shirt, and a ball cap, approached the front of my car and waved me into a parking spot to the left of the five-car garage. I set my Apple watch for an hour. I wasn't kidding about making a welfare check-in on Sarah and Brian. I wasn't completely gullible.

The house, three stories of used brick, was elegant and classic, with four columns holding the porte-cochere. I hopped out of my Suburban and started to lock 'er up, then all but laughed. I think my car would be safe here. I walked on the crushed shell driveway and up the massive marble steps to the two-story door. I didn't get a chance to get a hand on the slightly frightening knocker, (a brass rendition of a gargoyle), when a round-faced smiling woman opened the door.

"Ms. Ludlow?" She asked politely with a slight Spanish accent.

I smiled. "Yes."

She opened the door wider. "Come in, please," she said as she stepped back. I walked in. Wow, just WOW! The foyer was the size of my entire downstairs. There was a museum-worthy round table under the chandelier suspended from the two-story ceiling. The most exquisite crystal bowl was filled with 'just-picked from the garden' hydrangeas. The were blue, my favorite.

"Mr. Di'Rissi is waiting for you in his study. Please, follow me." She led me to the room on the right of the foyer. It was dark and cozy when we entered.

Mr. Di'Rissi rose from behind his desk and extended his hand. I took it, and was proud that I didn't shake, and looked him square in the eye. He didn't look scary. He was short, no taller than five-foot-six, and round. I bet his wife was a good cook.

"Mrs. Ludlow, or do you prefer 'Ms.'?" Was that said with just a wee bit of snark?

"Mrs. is fine." He circled his desk and indicated with his outstretched hand to join him at the seating area in front of a roaring fire. I sat on the edge of my seat. Well, so far, so good. I didn't see any plastic on the carpet, indicating Mr. Di'Rissi was going to shoot me on the spot. Wait, they usually took you for a ride when they were going to make you disappear. Right? Another delightful sign, there was a beautiful silver coffee service with yummy-looking pastries laid out on the table in front of me. That seemed very hospitable. Or…was it a last meal type of thing? Maybe he knew of my love of coffee? I was having cream in my coffee if it was my last meal, I promised myself.

"Kate," Mr. Di'Rissi said again, this time with slight concern in his voice, leading me to believe he had been trying to get my attention.

I turned my head to him. "I'm sorry, I'm not quite myself."

"Or are you nervous?" He laughed. I chose to laugh with him. Better, right?

"Relax, Mrs. Ludlow. I mean you no harm, as long as you can give me the same assurance." He didn't look so friendly, now.

I gulped but still met his gaze. "I mean you *absolutely* no harm, Mr. Di'Rissi," I said solemnly. But what I couldn't understand, *really*...was why I was still breathing. I knew too much, and he knew I knew too much.

"But..." He just looked at me, increasing my heart rate. Here it was. The moment of truth, the moment I would learn my fate.

He stood up, smoothed down the invisible creases in his very fine woolen slacks. He sure was a snappy dresser. He sauntered over to the fireplace's mantle and picked up a small silver frame. He walked back to me and placed it in my hands.

I looked down at the portrait in the frame. It was like looking in a mirror, if I was dressed in 1900s attire, that is. "Who?"

"My mother," he smiled, a real smile, and sat back down in the wing chair adjacent to where I sat on the sofa. "As you can see, I am going to have to rely on your word to keep your mouth shut. I just can't bring myself to harm a hair on your head." I knew my eyes had widened.

"Your beautiful daughter, Ellis, is it? Quite an unusual name for such a young beauty. Really doesn't look a whole lot like you, does she? While I'd hate to be such a brute, if I can't be guaranteed your complete discretion, I can't guarantee her...safety"

Oh my God! Was he just threatening my beloved daughter?

"Take a breath, Kate," his voice had lost all its charm, its friendliness. "As long as we can agree to mind our own business, all will be good, and all safe."

I felt very lucky. I'd be more than happy to agree to any terms he requested.

"Understood." I nodded my head once.

"Good!" The smile was back on his face, his jovialness restored. He stood and slapped his thighs as he did so. "But there is one more condition I'd like agreement to."

Oh God. This was it. The something that would be too much, that would put me into hiding...IF I could escape this fortress alive.

I gulped and raised my eyes to his. "Yes?"

"I would like to hire you to plan my Giselle's wedding. I really won't take no for an answer." His smile was predatory.

"It would be my great pleasure." I rose and extended my hand. He took it and placed his other hand over it.

"Delightful."

A Note from the Author

Mary Karnes is a real-life wedding planner with ten years' experience.

Acknowledgments

I would like to thank my family, especially my husband Ken, who is patient, kind, and supportive of my bucket list desire to be a traditionally published author. He is also a fabulous line editor.

And major kudos to my wonderful son-in-law, Rob, who has supplied potential storylines and read and edited each of my books.

Thank you to my children and grandchildren for understanding when Mom/Belle can't help or play because she is on deadline.

Thank you to Level Best Books, especially Shawn Simmons and Deb Well, for always having my back.

I am also grateful for the support from my fellow authors, Kim Davis, Celeste Connally, Korina Moss, Shari Randall, and Jane Willan.

Sisters in Crime National, New England, Connecticut and Los Angeles, you are appreciated.

About the Author

Mary Karnes, a college English major and former teacher, is the mother of four who raised her family through six corporate moves. She always dreamed of being an author and dabbled with writing throughout the years. Once the children were grown and out of the house, she started a wedding planning business, while simultaneously chasing her dream of being a traditionally published author. Her 'Wedding Planner Mystery Series' was born, with her business providing delicious subject matter for her books.

The first in the Wedding Planner Mystery Series, *Weddng Bride and Doom*, debuted in August 2023, and the second in the series, *Save The Fate,* was published in October 2024. Book Three, *Unveiled Secrets*, will publish in October 2025.

Mary resides in New England with her husband, Ken, and her mini-dachshund, Lucky. She is hard at work on something a little different, a stand-alone domestic thriller. Her door is a revolving one, with her children and grandchildren visiting frequently.

AUTHOR WEBSITE:

marykarnesauthor.com

SOCIAL MEDIA HANDLES:
@marykarnesauthor – Instagram
@marypkarnesweddings – Instagram
Marypkarnes – TikTok
Marypkarnesauthor – Facebook

Also by Mary Karnes

Wedding Bride and Doom

Save The Fate